WANTING THE PLAYER

RULES OF THE GAME
BOOK 2

HEATHER YOUNG-NICHOLS

Wanting the Player
Rules of the Game 2
USA Today Bestselling Author
Heather Young-Nichols

heatheryoungnichols.com

Forever Grayson

Forever London

Forever Lennox

Heavy Hitter

Pushing Daisies

Daisy

Van

Bonham

Daltrey

Mack

Courting Chaos

Cross

Ransom

Booker

Dixon

Finding Love

Making Her Mine

Making Him Hers

Harbor Point

Love by the Slice

Love by the Mile

Love by the Rules

Gambling on Love

Highest Bidder

Highest Stakes

Highest Reward

Holiday Bites

All I Want

All of Me

The Fallout Series

Last Good Thing

Last First Kiss

Last Chance Love

With J.A. Hardt

Bound by Magic

With Amelia J. Matthews

Dirt on the Diamond

After Office Hours: Seducing the Professor

CHAPTER 1
URBAN

This game is such bullshit sometimes.

Or that was what I loved to tell myself whenever I was in a slump or, honestly, at the most minor inconvenience. Baseball was in my blood, it should have been easy, yet I hadn't had a single hit in five fucking games. Walked like four times, but no hit.

Bob, the general manager, sat across from me in his office after I was called up here. Not usually the best sign but I wasn't worried. The place was too brown. Light brown at that, but it was like absolutely no imagination went into decorating the place. Bob was still in good shape, unlike most general managers. Most let themselves go once they got the job, if they ever had it in the first place, but not him. He worked out in the team facilities almost as much as the players did.

"You've been traded," Bob finally said.

"What?" I assumed this had to be a joke. Players didn't just get traded without knowing it was a possibility. Our agents should've at least been in on it, and I hadn't heard a peep from mine.

"Harden hasn't had a chance to call you." It wasn't a question, but it was the answer to my unspoken question.

Harden has been my agent for a few years now. Originally, he wasn't. My dad had pushed us to sign with one of his friends, but the minute I'd gotten drafted and left Kalamazoo, I'd changed agents. I wanted to cut all ties to my father, where baseball was concerned. Hell, I barely spoke to him outside of baseball, either.

Since Bob hadn't asked a question, I tightened my jaw so that I wouldn't give him the response I wanted to. A response that could cause me major problems.

I was pissed. But I was also in a slump, which made it hard to argue.

Did being in a slump mean that I was hearing from my brothers every fucking day? Yeah. It did. That was how this worked. Having all of your brothers also be professional ball players meant you caught shit when things weren't going the best. Like they never hit a slump. *Assholes.* But fuck. This was the next level.

"I'm sorry to see you go, Briggs, but it had to be done." Bob sat back and pressed his fingers together under his chin like he was some villain in a movie, and I had yet to utter a word. "You're valuable."

And to them, I was a commodity.

"Right." I cleared my throat to prevent myself from unleashing the torrent of words that were sitting there waiting for him to hear like little friends listening to some gossip. "Where am I going?"

Bob took a deep breath. How he did it made me think he was biding time or soaking up these last seconds, leaving my stomach tight. Either way, I wasn't going to like the answer.

There was only one team that I thought would have him acting that way.

"We're getting a pitcher, Sands, and three prospects," he said as if defending the decision without telling me what it was. "Two of those are pitchers. You know that's our weakness right now."

Through clenched teeth, I asked again, "Where am I going?"

He ran a hand across his chin before saying, "Kalamazoo."

"Fuck that," I spat, unable to keep it in any longer as I launched from the chair. "I'm not going to Kalamazoo."

"You are," he countered. "You don't have a right of refusal in your contract. Maybe that's something you can work into your next one. Your contract expires at the end of this year. You had to know this was coming. You're expensive, and we have a great backup first baseman." His gaze met mine. "Or a great first baseman now. He's not you. You don't have to tell me that, but he's the next best thing."

"Kalamazoo? Really, Bob?" This feeling that I was about to come out of my skin surged. If I didn't get out of there soon, I'd do something I'd regret. Something really stupid. "Every single person who knows anything knows that's the last place I want to be."

"They approached us." He shook his head. "It's a deal we couldn't afford to refuse."

"Yeah, right." I got to the door, yanked it open, and let it slam against the wall as I left.

"Get it in your next contract," he called out. He

couldn't see the middle finger I raised over my shoulder at him.

Yeah. Fuck that. My next contract would be negotiated with my damn mother. Scratch that. I'd have Harden get me somewhere else next year.

I could do one year in Kalamazoo. One year. I could do anything for a year, right? It's not even an entire year. The part that wouldn't suck was that, for the rest of the season, I'd be playing with two of my brothers. That, I could get behind. Being back under my father's thumb… wasn't fucking going to happen.

After leaving Bob's office, I stomped my way back down to the clubhouse. If I was off the team, I needed to clean out my locker for the next guy to take. That was how it was in baseball. I blamed this slump. Maybe if I'd had a hit, they wouldn't have traded me.

Everyone hit a slump. It'd been five games. Nothing more. My bat had cooled, that was all. I had a plan to fix it. Now it didn't matter because I was going to be on a plane to Kalamazoo today.

This was the worst fucking part of baseball.

I was a twenty-four-year-old grown-ass man. Which meant I was just being a whiny bitch about this whole thing. But our dad was an asshole and rode the four of us boys harder than a pack of mules on the baseball conveyer belt that he'd set up.

The door to the clubhouse slammed against the wall when I opened it more aggressively than I'd needed to. Luckily, the clubhouse had mostly cleared out, except for Jared, our second baseman. He jumped in surprise.

He was a few inches shorter than me and had the blond hair, blue eyed thing that women swooned for.

"Tough game," he said as he pulled his shirt down over his chest.

"Yeah." I stopped at my locker, which was next to his. Ours were large, though, not like the shit in the locker room in high school or college.

I'd been drafted to a minor league team in California—the other side of the country from my dad, which had been fine with me. However, I'd been traded to Florida before I'd gotten called up. Still the other end of the country from Michigan, just a different end. Our team wasn't the best in the league, but it was building. I was supposed to be part of that build. Most of the time, I was one of the best players on the team, even if I wasn't the best player among the brothers. However, that was a hard comparison to make. We'd played together since we could walk. The best of the brothers changed with the day.

"What are you so pissy about?"

"I got traded," I said flatly. Jared opened his mouth to respond, but I didn't let him. "Want to guess to where?"

"No fucking way."

"My feelings exactly." I yanked a duffle big enough to put my shit in out of my locker. "Bob said they made the team an offer they couldn't refuse."

Jared's eyes grew wider. "Fuck. It better have been good."

"You're getting Sands and three prospects. I think he said two are pitchers." Not that I necessarily paid attention given the rage making me hear my heart pulse in my ears as I sat across from him.

"Oh, shit." His tone told me that he, too, felt it was an offer they couldn't refuse. If I looked at it strictly from a baseball point of view, it was. This team needed pitchers. It was their weak spot, and getting potentially three while only having to sacrifice me—it made sense.

Didn't mean I liked it.

"Did you tell your agent that Kalamazoo was the one place you never wanted to go?"

I nodded. "It's not in my contract, though. I don't get to refuse."

"Right." He blew out a breath. "Well, fuck. Drinks tonight? Like a going away? When do you leave?"

As if Jared had summoned the gods, my phone vibrated. After pulling it out of my pocket, I opened the message. It was from Harden, my agent… and there wouldn't be time for drinks. There rarely ever was in a situation like this.

"Plane leaves in four hours," I told him. "I have to go pack up the shit I need to take with me today."

"Right." He reached a hand out for me to shake, and I took it, and then we pulled in for a guy hug. He patted my back, then hoisted his bag onto his shoulder and left me to clean out my damn life.

Minutes later, I was walking out to my car, knowing that the next time I was inside this stadium, it would be as a visitor. A weird feeling settled in my chest. This was the only major league park that had been home my entire career. Granted, that had only been, like, four years. Where I was headed was likely the source of the tightness in my chest, not where I was leaving. I loved it here, sure, but leaving had always been a possibility, and now it was a reality.

Damn, I wished I had time to drive my car up to Michigan, but no. When you were traded, your ass was on a plane that day. Luckily, the team I was leaving would send movers to pack up my apartment and ship everything I didn't take with me today—including my car.

Two hours later, I had a couple of bags packed with my clothes and baseball shit since that went with me. Players didn't break in new gloves just because they'd moved. Then I had a carry-on and dropped my keys on the counter with the list I made of what needed to be shipped and where. I put my brother Brooks's address because I had no idea where I was going to be living and his house had a large enough garage as well as a basement to store everything when it showed up. The Knights would have somewhere for me to stay temporarily.

Whatever. It was my first time doing this, but hopefully not my last and I wasn't leaving behind anything I cared about. There was a model, Analise, that I'd hooked up with for a while but even that had ended.

The rideshare took me to the airport, where I checked my bags and then waited to board. The airport was so busy that I made sure to get to my gate so I wouldn't miss the flight. Harden had gotten me first-class tickets—probably funded by my mother personally and not the team—and I fought the urge to call and rip Harden a new one. No. It was better that we texted for now, so I ignored his call when he tried getting in touch.

This wasn't his fault. He'd asked me if I wanted the right to refuse a trade, but I'd said *no*. I'd been focused on the bigger payday that had come with the contract my team had offered. At that time, I'd been in the minor leagues, so the idea of being on the Knights hadn't been front and center.

Instead, I texted him that things were fine. I didn't want to talk right now and really didn't want to take my anger out on him.

But we'd do better next time, and at least there was a provision in my contract that meant I'd be getting paid more with the trade. Any team I was traded to had to up my pay.

That only lessened the blow a little bit.

Once I was settled on the plane, I tried to relax. It might be the last moment of relaxation I got. First class wasn't sold out so aside from having plenty of legroom, I had some peace.

The Knights weren't a bad team. In fact, they

were a pretty great team. It was also my grandpa's team. Those were the positives.

Grandpa had bought the Knights a long time ago. Before my mom had been born, even. Since she was an only child, he'd had his sights set on her taking it over when he was done. I'd thought that meant when he died, but he hadn't been well and was too old to keep up with all of the day-to-day shit. So Mom had taken over quite a few years ago.

Whether she'd supported my dad's quest for us to be ballplayers, I didn't know. At the very least, she didn't object to it and she was proud of us when we did well. She probably would've also have been proud of us doing well in any area we chose. Luckily for him, my brothers and I loved playing. He saw it as a feather in his cap that we had all been good enough to be drafted.

Brooks, the oldest at twenty-seven, the catcher, had been drafted right onto the Knights and was still there. Once one of us was on the team, it would be damn near impossible to get traded. I was going to have to try like hell at the end of this season. Brooks was happy there. He'd told my dad to fuck off, and Dad didn't play a part of any of our careers anymore, unless you counted getting us all onto the Knights. That was his dream these days.

Though I couldn't be sure, Mom probably wouldn't do it if it didn't make sense for the team. She was a master at putting Dad in his place about the business. She was running it. Not him. Period.

Then Silas ended up on the Knights a couple of years ago. He was twenty-five, a second baseman, which they'd needed after their veteran had gotten a career-ending injury. Silas had also become the first of us to find their forever person. He was with Amity Kincaid now, a woman we'd known since we were all kids.

My younger brother, Cobb, was a pitching powerhouse. He was insanely good and would be the most resistant to fulfilling Dad's dream of having his legacy all on the same team. Dad was in the Hall of Fame. Apparently, that wasn't enough.

Our little sister, Camden, had come along and ruined his plan of having all boys who played base-ball. He loved her… I thought he loved all of us… He just had a weird way of showing it.

Fuck. This flight gave me too much time to think.

Almost as soon as I stepped off the plane and headed to baggage claim, my phone vibrated in my pocket. I should've predicted my mother was probably tracking the damn plane so she could call as soon as I touched the ground.

"Hey," I answered.

"I know you're pissed," she told me. "I'm sorry about the way this happened, but I saw an opportunity and jumped. I also didn't want to give you the chance to say no."

I sighed. Mom was a gem. She wanted us to be happy but also had a business to run. Besides, if she'd asked me and I said no, would she have listened? The mom side would have but I didn't think the GM of the Kalamazoo Knights side could. "I know, Mom."

"Are you happy to be home? Even a little?" she asked as I pulled a bag off the conveyor belt.

"No," I told her honestly. "It'll be nice to see you and Camden, but no. You know this is the last place I wanted to play." My second suitcase came racing toward me. I grabbed that one and pulled it off, too.

"We're a pretty good team, Urban. You can't let the strain between you and your dad hold you back on anything." She wasn't wrong but it was the last thing I wanted to hear.

I turned and almost ran right into a man in a

black suit. "Fuck." The word tumbled out of my mouth. Mom chuckled on the other end.

"I'm assuming Emmet found you."

"I'm thinking he did. You need to make him wear a bell."

"Good. He can get you to the apartment. I got you one not too far from Brook's house. I thought you'd like that." Papers shuffled on the other end. "Emmet has a key, and it's already furnished. We can change anything you don't like. I rented it for you but it you want to stay there, we'll switch everything to your name, so it's yours. I know you won't want to keep it in mine."

She was right. Part of having those boundaries with my dad was keeping things separate. Not that any of us cared about the money. We'd grown up with more than anyone needed and got paid obscene amounts to play a game. Money wasn't the issue.

"So it's not the team apartment that you always use?" Because the Knight had a place that they rented for scouts, visitors, players who abruptly got traded and needed a little while to get everything in place. It was basically a Kalamazoo Knight AirBNB.

"No. This is separate because I want you to be comfortable."

I snorted. "That's special treatment, Mother."

She sighed her frustration at me. "Urban… you're right. It is. Sue me. I wanted to do something nice for my kid. If you don't want it—"

I snickered. "I'm sure it'll be fine."

"Until the end of the season, right?" My mom knew us all so well. She knew us as men and as players, and she'd automatically realize I'd want to move to another team at the end of the year, given that it was unlikely I'd be traded twice a season, even if it was early. Still, I remained silent. There was no need to confirm what she already knew.

She sighed again. When we were kids, she sighed and pinched the bridge of her nose a lot. "Well, enjoy playing with your brothers the rest of the season," she told me. "And go get settled. I'll see you tomorrow."

Which meant she'd be at the ballpark.

After getting my things in the car, Emmet maneuvered us through traffic. The Knights had a night game, which meant traffic was crazy in that area, which happened to not be far from the building Mom had put me in.

This would at least give me a few hours before

my brothers descended because there was no doubt that would be happening tonight.

It also gave me time to think things through and make some plans.

Like not creating a life here that I wouldn't be able to walk away from in a few months.

Because leaving Kalamazoo was now my longer-term priority.

CHAPTER 2
EVERLY

*H*ow in the hell did I accumulate so much shit during a single school year? Every fall, I start out with only what I thought I needed. Then by the end of the school year, it became boxes and boxes of shit.

Also… I hated that I had to pack up my room every year if I wanted my things to be there again in the fall. The school moved our rooms randomly sometimes, and when the janitorial staff cleaned, things got thrown away. There was no way for them to know what was good to keep and what was trash.

Once I had my last box in my car, I shut the hatch and left for the summer.

Most people believe that teachers get a vacation in the summer, and for some, that would be true.

For me… my summer job started the following Monday.

For the last two summers, I'd worked at a summer camp. It seemed to be a natural extension of what I loved to do. Teach.

As if she knew I was thinking about camp starting on Monday, my best friend, Jade, called. Thank goodness for Bluetooth.

"Did you know I was thinking about you?" I asked instead of greeting her.

"I assume you always are." She giggled. I had to laugh too. The last thing Jade would do was think that the world revolved around her. That woman was as selfless as they came, and sometimes, I felt selfish in comparison. "Are you done packing?"

"I am. I'll have to go through all of this because I'm sure I don't need everything in these boxes, but that sounds like a *future Everly* problem." Because that was how I handled anything I didn't want to deal with most of the time.

My bandwidth typically only allowed me to deal with whatever *emergency* was in front of me. They were never my emergencies.

"That's what I think too. I packed up all of my supplies, knowing that some of them are going to be dried out when school starts back up." As the art teacher, Jade usually ordered supplies for the next year at the end of this one so she could hit the ground running. The worst thing you could do was have a bunch of high schoolers you were in charge of with nothing to do.

"So we're done."

"Until Monday," she reminded me.

Right. Camp. I loved working at the camp, and so did she. It was rewarding in a new way. However, not working for three months also sounded like fun.

As I pulled into my apartment complex, Jade hopped out of her car carrying a pizza box from the place closest to my apartment complex. This thoughtfulness was part of the reason she was my best friend.

I ended the call without saying anything then cut the engine so that I could get out.

"What are you doing here?" I asked.

She shrugged. "I thought we could plan the weekend and what we're going to do at camp next week." Then she held the pizza up to me. "And I thought you might be hungry."

I was starving, actually.

I only carried one box of school supplies into my apartment and would get the other later.

My apartment wasn't huge because I didn't need

anything too large. When we walked in the door, it was into the living room with an attached dining area. To the right was the storage unit where I'd drop this box and forget about it for a couple of months and to the left was the kitchen. Barely bigger than a galley kitchen, it met my needs. On the other side was a small hallway that led to my bedroom and the bathroom.

With my touches, or rather Jade's since she was the artist, the place was modern and funky but cozy.

Jade went to the couch in the living room while I grabbed us plates and drinks.

The first bite was what I imagined heaven to taste like. It was so good that I moaned.

"That must be some seriously good pizza," Jade told me before taking a bite for herself. "Oh, shit. It *is* seriously good pizza." Which, it always was but today, it just hit the spot.

"Thanks for bringing it." I took another bite before pushing her harder. "But seriously, why did you wait for me here today?"

She shrugged. "I figured we have a few days before starting another job, so we should take advantage of it. Want to go to Chicago?"

I snorted. "You know you don't have to work at

the camp. You could take your summers off. Travel. Do whatever people with money do."

Jade's family had money. They weren't going to be owning an island anytime soon—that I knew of —but she had a trust fund from her grandparents and her parents had money. It was enough that I knew she taught high school art because she felt it was her calling. She could've probably lived a life of luxury if she'd wanted to.

She rolled her eyes. "I could, but then how would you survive high school a second time?"

Now I had to laugh. Jade had been my best friend since we'd been in kindergarten. She knew how much I hated high school, but mostly because everyone would fall all over my brother all the time, and I could never tell if someone was talking to me —or being nice—because they liked me or because they wanted a way in with my brother.

Except Jade.

"OK." She slapped her hands together. "What does camp look like this year?"

I shrugged. "You know I don't make lesson plans for camp. I'm not in charge. I'm not even a counselor. I just run a few programs, and they'll tell me which ones when I get there on Monday. I know it'll be the baseball camp again because I run that every year—"

"And it was your idea."

"Right. But other than that… I don't know. How many classes are you teaching?"

"Just one this year. Last year's attendance for all the art classes wasn't the best, so we thought just one this year would drum up more interest. But I'm also overseeing a couple of independent study students from last year who are already beyond what I'll be teaching this year. So I'll be around."

Which suited me just fine.

"I can't wait for the hot baseball players to arrive at camp," she said while wiggling her eyebrows up and down suggestively.

This was a day camp, but one section—usually the first—included a baseball rotation. So, for weeks, my group would be focused on baseball. Then there were other activities that kids signed up for during those weeks.

For example, there was an arts rotation in which Jade taught painting. There are other things that they did, and this was all in the morning. They then got to do an afternoon rotation, and there was time for the fun stuff of swimming and hiking. Usually, I did baseball in the morning, and then after lunch, I took my group either swimming or hiking and then we had other activities to do.

I groaned at the thought of which players would be coming.

"I can wait," I told her flatly.

"You could find the love of your life in a professional baseball player, Everly."

"Not a chance," I told her immediately. "Sex… absolutely. But a relationship? Never again. Like with baseball, three strikes, and I'm out."

Jade sighed and took another slice of pizza. "You had a string of bad luck. And I can't believe you hardly know anything about baseball."

"Bad luck?" I asked with outrage. "Number one: Slept with my sister. Number two: Slept with another teacher at the school. And number three: Tried to put my belongings up for sale on the marketplace. Never again. And I don't teach baseball, I supervise. You don't have to know how to play for that. Hence the players coming."

That sister, I still didn't talk to. My brother and I were sort of close, but my other sister only ever wanted money, so I stayed away as much as possible. And my parents, who were somehow still married even though they shouldn't have been, thought that it was my responsibility to help everyone in the family whenever they needed it simply because I made more money than they did.

I was a teacher. How much did they think I made?

"The kids love the players showing up. You have to be excited for that."

"I'm not. And you know why. Maybe I will be once I know that Bryson Madden isn't going to be one of them."

Jade cringed. "Yeah. It'd be best if he didn't come again. You did get him to stop calling, though. That's something."

I shook my head. "Only because I blocked his ass."

Bryson Madden was a member of the Kalamazoo Knights, and he'd been one of the volunteers last summer. We always got a few players to come because the camp was affiliated with the Briggs family, who owned the team. It had been a passion project of the owner's wife. Apparently, she'd grown up pretty poor and wanted to give back to the community, so she'd started this camp. Then she died, and none of the other family typically helped, with the exception of Camden, the only daughter in the latest generation. She'd said she'd been a counselor since she'd been sixteen and she volunteered every summer. That Knights owner was too old to do much other than donate money. His daughter ran the team now.

"Hooking up with Madden last summer was a colossal mistake," I told her. "The sex wasn't good enough to result in him feeling attached. I'm not doing that again."

"Yeah, he did become a stage-five clinger, didn't he?" Jade downed half of her pop before speaking again.

This was our thing. We hung out and talked, and that was enough. Sure, sometimes, we went on adventures, but this right here was the bread and butter of our friendship.

"Who would've thought the manly professional baseball player would get clingy?" she asked.

"Hey." I sat up straighter. "They put their pants on one leg at a time, just like the rest of us. They're just more expensive pants."

We fell into a fit of giggles. Once we'd calmed down, we put in a rom-com about how easy it was to chase a guy away and of course the main characters fell in love. For a woman who didn't believe in romance, I sure did love the Hallmark Christmas movies and romantic comedies.

Jade and I were like sisters. We could be in the

same room—not talking—while still having an entire conversation. We were both on our phones sending each other memes the entire time too.

At nearly midnight, I let out a loud yawn with a big stretch. It was time for bed.

"Are you staying or going?" I asked because she'd stayed here more times than I could count, just as I had at her apartment. Admittedly, her apartment was bigger and nicer. She even had a guest bedroom.

"Staying. We're shopping tomorrow." She stretched her legs across the couch and smiled up at me.

I groaned. Shopping wasn't my favorite thing to do.

"What?" she countered. "You need summer clothes. Are you going to wear all of those skirts at camp?"

"No. But I have clothes from last year. It's not like I've grown." As a matter of fact, I'd stopped growing at around fourteen, maybe younger. Which meant I wasn't very tall, and I was athletically built, though I was too thin, according to my mother, and everything else was… proportional, though I thought my ass was slightly too big. Jade was always quick to point out that it wasn't *big*, but toned.

She, on the other hand, was barely taller than me and much thinner. She was naturally small because that woman could put back the chili cheese fries with the best of us. She always said that one day, she'd have to focus on food and exercise because her metabolism wasn't going to last forever.

"That's right. You haven't grown, but you deserve to buy new things." Now she stood and came over to me to rest her hands on my shoulders. "I understand that all of your money goes to savings because you never want it to be like how you grew up. I get that. I was there, remember. But you've got a fat savings and need to treat yourself once in a while." When she headed back to the couch, she snapped her fingers. "Oh, and we're getting massages. That's my treat, so you can't turn it down."

I grumbled my way to my bedroom, though I couldn't deny that a massage would feel really good right about now.

In the morning, Jade insisted we get breakfast first. Fine by me. I was starving. Then we headed out to her favorite store. I liked to say the clothes were out of my price range, but she hadn't been wrong last night. I could afford to splurge every now and then.

When it came time to try on some clothes, I pulled my hair into a messy bun. The stylist called it "caramel blonde," and I loved it. Jade's was a much lighter blonde, which suited her so well. But for now, I needed that hair out of my way. It fell to the middle of my back in waves—most of the time—but when summer hit, the messy bun because my second best friend. After Jade.

"What do you think?" she asked when I stepped out in a retro bikini. This was not for camp. I'd wear a one piece for that.

"I kind of love it." I stepped in front of the full-length mirror outside the dressing room. There was one inside, but Jade insisted on seeing everything because she knew I'd talk myself out of buying anything if left alone.

"Your boobs look amazing in that." She was wearing one with less coverage. I had one like that and loved it, too, but this retro style was amazing.

And my boobs looked fantastic.

Then I saw something in the mirror that made my entire body tense like it was now on high alert.

Unfortunately, he saw me, too.

I hurried into the dressing room and changed. Jade did, too, even thought she had no idea why. All she would've seen was my reaction and them me hurrying to change. She wouldn't ask questions until we were done. The last thing I wanted was to be caught in something like a bikini with him around. It wasn't until we were headed to the cash register with our choices that she understood.

"This is a coincidence, right?" she whispered, and I nodded. It had to be.

"Everly, funny running into you here," Bryson Madden said, causing Jade and me to stop and turn. Bryson was a big guy though not the biggest in baseball. He was taller than us, of course, but that wasn't hard and he had blonde hair with brown eyes. That *boy next door* kind of vibe.

"Yeah. Funny. We both buy clothing. What a coincidence," I said. Jade and I slipped into the checkout line, and he got in right behind us. I wasn't even sure he had anything to buy with him. Probably he just wanted to pester me.

He needed to go away.

"I was just thinking about you." No. He wasn't. "Change your mind yet?"

"Nope." That was the explanation he was going to get. *No* was a full sentence. One that he seemed to not want to understand.

"Listen, I—"

"What the fuck are you doing here?" another

male voice asked. I had to look around to see that he was talking to Bryson.

"Had to pick something up," Bryson told him. "Ran into a friend."

I snorted. We weren't friends. But when Bryson reached out and ran his hand down my arm, I flinched and stepped away, causing this other man's brows to furrow. Bryson's friend was as hot as they came. He was tall, with dark hair and brooding eyes. His features were pinches and his eyebrows were narrowed. It made me think he wasn't all that happy to be here.

"Uh…" Bryson's friend scratched at his jaw, like he was about to say something uncomfortable, but then he locked gazes with me and pointed toward the register. "They're ready for you."

Thank the universe because standing next to a man I'd hooked up almost a year ago but now wouldn't leave me alone wasn't how I'd planned to use my Saturday.

I scurried off and did my transaction.

When Jade and I got out to the parking lot, we heard someone call out, "Hey." We turned, and it was Bryson's friend jogging toward us.

I groaned as I dropped my bag in the trunk. I wasn't afraid he had a nefarious plan but annoyed that anyone having to do with Bryson was going to take up my time. Though if someone was… I think this guy would've been who I would've chosen myself.

"Was he bothering you?" the man asked. Out in the sun, it was everything I could do to not drool over this guy. His build and the way he carried himself, told me he absolutely was a baseball player. Strong muscles, long not bulky, broad shoulders, thicker thighs…

Why was this my type? It was my own fault I ended up getting fucked over, given that this cocky thing they all had going on was exactly *my* thing.

"He's always a bother," I said.

He furrowed his brows. "Are you friends?"

Jade laughed loudly. "Not even close. He's obsessed with her or something."

I held up a hand to stop her from saying anything else. "I wouldn't go that far, but if you could get your friend to leave me alone, that'd be great. I'd take the help."

The guy nodded twice and said, "Done." Then he walked away.

"That was weird," Jade said as we both stood watching him walk away. It was a glorious sight.

Too bad I wouldn't hook up with baseball players anymore. Too intense.

"It was, but if he can get Bryson off my back, I'll take weird."

She nudged me with her shoulder. "You must be really good in bed."

This definitely made me laugh. "I am. I really am."

In reality, I wasn't that conceited. Bryson just thought we'd clicked when we hadn't. Not even enough to be a regular hookup.

But his friend… *that* was someone I could see being a regular sex partner. No strings, just fun.

If only he weren't a baseball player.

CHAPTER 3
URBAN

'd been able to avoid my father for three days.

Three. Glorious. Days.

As expected, my brothers came to my apartment the night I'd arrived in Kalamazoo. Mom had come over the next morning on her way to the office, which meant she'd been alone. But fuck if Dad didn't walk into the clubhouse when I was getting dressed for batting practice.

So far, everyone had been very welcoming. The team had acted happy that I was there and since I'd gotten two hits in both of the games I'd played, my slump was over. Or so I hoped.

"Urban." Dad greeted me as if I hadn't seen

him standing there. There was no denying that he was my father. Though all of us boys had gotten taller than him, even if only by an inch or two, he had the same dark hair and eyes that we had.

For a lot of the guys, Dad was still a big deal. As a baseball player, he was a legend. Unfortunately for my siblings and me, we knew just how much of an asshole he could be. Well, everyone probably knew that, given his cockiness when he played. Professional athletes were the best in the world at what they did, which meant we'd earned a bit of an ego.

The problem was that Dad had never learned to control his.

"Conrad." I greeted him back, knowing that one of his kids calling him by his first name irritated him. It always had.

"Your mother's happy to have you back home."

I snorted. "I'm sure she is. I'm sure *you* are."

He sighed. "Let's go out into the hall."

Fine by me. The last thing I wanted was for an argument to break out in front of my new teammates. Not exactly the impression that I wanted to make.

Dad left the clubhouse first with me following

behind. It wasn't until we were several feet from the door that we stopped and he turned to me.

"I *am* happy to have you back in town. Not sure why you would think I wouldn't be." He folded his arms over his chest the way he did when he was trying to intimidate another player. But he forgot that he didn't intimidate any of us anymore and hadn't since we were little kids. "I just wanted to touch base because I'm sure your ass is gonna be on fire trying to get out of here as soon as your contract expires. I think I have some ideas that might help keep you here once the season ends."

"The fuck you do. There's nothing that's going to keep me here at the end of this season."

"You're sure of that?"

"Yeah, because the last thing I'm going to do is let you have any say in my career. You might have put us all through an assembly line to get us to where we are, but these are our lives now. We're grown men. You get no say." I took a step closer to him just to show that he wasn't intimidating me, if that was his intent. "You might've gotten me here, but that's where this ends."

"You being here was your mother's decision. She runs this team and doesn't clear her choices with me. You know your grandpa and mom have wanted you all on the Knights since they knew we had boys."

That much was true, but everything I said still stood. Dad was desperate to show us all that he could manage our careers better than we could because he'd been through it. It would've been nice if we'd had the guiding hand that should've come with our dad being a professional baseball player, but we didn't get that. We got the heavy-handed, *my way is the only way* bullshit.

No. I wasn't doing that.

"We done?" I asked. He nodded, so I turned and went back into the clubhouse.

It was only a minute before we were all filing out for batting practice. Once we were out there, it was a lot of waiting around for our turns. We laughed and smack-talked whoever was at the plate while we did it.

That was until I had an older brother on each side of me. They'd done that shit all the time when we'd been kids. Box me in so I knew I had nowhere to go. It didn't fucking work as adults but they still did it.

"Looks like you had an intense conversation with Dad," Brooks said as he watched the batter take a swing. I didn't bother looking over at my oldest brother. We'd grown up looking alike, Though brooks was slightly broader than the rest of us. That was what made him a good catcher.

"What else is new?" I asked.

"Can we give you some advice?" Silas asked, as if I had the option to say *no*. "Don't let him bug you. It takes too much energy." Silas and Brooks looked more like each other the way Cobb and I did. It was like Mom had two sets of twins though years apart. Genetics were weird.

"What?" I swung my head around to look at him. "What the fuck are you talking about? You both butt heads with that man."

Silas nodded, but he wasn't looking at me. "We do, but you're agro about it. I thought you were going to fist-fight him in the hallway. Just learn to push back when you need to and figure out what you can let go."

"I do that," I told him, then I tried to find what he was looking at. "Today was special because he was coming to do exactly what I thought he was coming to do."

"And what's that?"

"Butt into my career. Look…" I turned back to him once I'd noticed that he was looking at Amity as she worked on a tablet on her lap. Amity wasn't very tall, thin while still being curvy. She was sitting there in a dress of some kind with her feet propped on the back of a seat and an iPad on her lap. "I don't want to be here. Neither of you want to be here. Yet here we fucking are."

"Hey," Brooks snapped. "That's baseball. You could be here, you could play for Alaska. It's how it works."

"Alaska doesn't even have a team."

"Not the point," he countered. "Just block out most of the shit he says. When he really oversteps, that's when you go for the throat. Until then, you're here. Mom's glad you're here. We're glad you're here, and the Knights are a really fucking good team." He rested his hands on my shoulders. "And we just got better. Besides, I love it here." Though that hadn't always been the case. "There are some perks to being the GM's kid. And I'd bet my right nut that wild horses couldn't drag Silas away because this is where Amity is."

"That's true," Silas offered. "I mean, I think she'd leave with me but... that's not a guarantee and I wouldn't want her to give up her job for me."

He was right. I couldn't let my relationship with my parents affect this. Baseball was my job and I loved it. So everything else would have to fall away.

"So." I turned to Silas. "When do we get to hang out with Amity? I'd like to find out what the hell she's thinking being with you."

Brooks groaned. "Please don't. He was a whiny little bitch when they weren't together."

"No, I wasn't," Silas countered, but then he turned to me. "Whenever you want. Nothing you'll say will change anything."

It was weird to think of Silas so committed to a woman. That was new and something he'd never done before. Amity was his best friend's little sister. She'd been around us since we'd all been kids. Then Jayce had died and Silas had withdrawn because he'd blamed himself and thought Amity would hate him. It hadn't been until this year that he'd finally forgiven himself and only once Amity had assured him it'd just been an accident.

Fuck. It'd been tough watching her mourn her brother and being confused because she'd also lost Silas and their other friend—as well as my new teammate—Jenner. Those two looked out for her, but at a distance after Jayce had died.

Since Amity was only a year younger than me, I'd seen it every day until I'd graduated.

"We'll see about that," I told him, but there wasn't any intent behind it. I'd never do something I knew would tear one of my brothers up.

After batting practice, we were back in the clubhouse with about an hour and a half until game time. This was when we grabbed something to eat if we needed to, rested up, and got dressed for the game.

I was eating a protein bar and scrolling through my phone while the rest of the team had conversations. I had Brooks to my left and Silas next to him and then Jenner.

"Has Camden been blowing up your phone?" I asked anyone who wanted to listen, but mostly my brothers.

"No. What does she want?" Brooks drained half a bottle of water then wiped the back of his hand across his mouth.

"She's all over me to volunteer at Grandpa's camp for their baseball camp."

Silas laughed loudly. "Of course she is. Watch it. She's going to show up on your door step with a schedule and a plan. You won't be able to say *no*."

"Don't say *no*," Brooks added. "It's actually pretty fun and the kids get all starstruck. When you teach them something, that's a memory they're going to have forever."

I furrowed my brows. "I'll do it. This might be the only year I'm here to volunteer. She just hadn't given me a chance to answer." My phone vibrated again. "Fuck."

Yup. It was my sister again.

I quickly tapped out *fucking stop i'll' do it i was always going to do it.*

She just responded with a thumbs-up emoji. What the fuck?

That night, after a long game that had gone extra innings, I was looking forward to going to bed. Before I had a chance, there was a knock on my door. I knew who it was going to be before I even opened it since there weren't many people who knew that I lived here.

"Camden," I said as I swung it open. She breezed in like this was her place, her brown hair was hanging loose over her shoulders. It wasn't very long, she'd gotten it cut since the last time I'd seen her but it still fell past her shoulders.

"Brother, dear. I'm so glad you decided to participate in camp this year." She turned toward me and had a satisfied grin on her face as her hazel eyes danced with mischief. As if she'd ever really believed that I wouldn't.

I might've been an asshole to our dad, but I would do anything for my siblings and them for me. "Did I have a choice?"

"No." She chuckled as she pulled a folded-up piece of paper out of her purse. "This is the schedule. Baseball camp starts Monday and follows your schedule. Obviously, none of you can be there when you're traveling and not all of you go every year."

"How many from the team volunteer?" I took the schedule from her and unfolded it so I could see what it looked like. Not terrible. It was two hours two to three times a week for me.

"Ten. We don't need more than that and we alternate days. So this week, you'll be there Monday, Wednesday, and Friday. I put you in the group with Brooks, Silas, and Jenner. The kids are going to love having the brothers there. But then next week, you'll only be there Tuesday and Thursday. And it's only a few weeks."

"Sounds good." I glanced up at her. "You know, you could've emailed this."

She bit the corner of her cheek the way she did when she was trying not to smile. It was a complete failure. "I know I could've, but then I wouldn't get to see my big brother."

"You can come over anytime, Camden." But I glanced at the clock. "Except right now."

Her smile slowly slid from her face and she took a step toward me. "Is there a woman here?" she whispered.

I furrowed my brows. "No. I was going to bed."

"Alone?"

I pushed her hard enough to move her, but not hard enough to move her much. "Get the fuck out of here with that. No. We have a day game tomorrow. Sunday, remember? And I want to go see Grandpa before."

"I'll meet you there," she volunteered. "He'll be happy to hear about camp, too."

I shook my head. "You don't have to meet me."

Her face scrunched up, like she'd just smelled something awful. "I need to see Grandpa, anyway."

"Fine. I'll be there at eight. I have to get to the field early to talk to Madden. Didn't have time to do it today."

"Talk to Madden?" she asked. "Are you two friends?"

"Fuck no."

"Then what?"

"I saw him at the store yesterday talking to this woman. She looked uncomfortable, so I made sure she got to the register while I distracted him." I shrugged. "I don't know. It gave me a weird vibe."

"Yeah, that guy gives me a weird vibe too."

Rage pulsed through my blood. "Did he do something to you? *Try* to do something with you?"

She winced and waved her hands in the air as if she was trying to land a plane. "God no, Cujo. Jesus Christ. You look like you're about to kill someone. It's just a general gut feeling and I always trust my gut."

"Well, he better fucking not. Or any of the other guys on the team."

She snorted. "You know I'm vehemently against dating any baseball players, right? Probably any professional athletes of any kind."

"Yeah, well that shit changes, but for you, it shouldn't."

Camden wrapped her arms around my waist, so I put my own arms around her shoulders in a big hug, holding her rightly.

"It's not going to change," she mumbled against my chest. "Promise."

At least with that, I could sleep tonight.

In the morning, she was waiting outside of

Grandpa's assisted living facility with a coffee in each hand. When I approached, she held one out to me before I even had to ask.

"Thanks," I told her before heading in.

Grandpa's place looked like a high-dollar country club—it should've. It cost enough. We got to his room and knocked. Normally, I'd have been worried he was asleep, but Mom told me he got up at five every morning. It was like he couldn't let go of his old schedule after he'd retired.

"There you are," he answered, as if we were late or something. I hadn't even told him we'd been coming. He moved slowly away from the door so that we could enter his room, which was set up like a large studio apartment.

Granpa didn't act any different than he had my entire childhood. He was just a lot slower at the things he did. He couldn't live alone anymore and I saw the oxygen machine over in the corner. He didn't need it all the time but the bad lungs he'd dealt with since he was a kid gave him trouble sometimes. More recently than they had before.

"Did you know we were coming?" I asked.

"Your mother told me on our call last night." That was right. Mom called him every night and every morning. "What brings you by?"

Grandpa had brown hair when he was younger but now it was all silver. His face wrinkled with time but he still had a kind, gentle smile. He also wasn't very tall to begin with and it was like time had put him on the high heat setting of the dryer. He had to have lost a few inches. Once I hit a growth spirt, I felt like a giant next to him.

"Haven't seen you since I've been back," I told him, sitting across the table from him. Grandpa always preferred sitting with us at the table rather than the couch.

"Can I get either of you a drink?"

"We're good," Camden replied for the both of us.

"I'm so glad you're back in Kalamazoo." That had to be for me.

"He's not happy to be here, though," Camden offered up, so I scowled at her. The old man didn't need to know that. Leave it to her to pull no punches.

"He will be," Grandpa said with such confidence that I almost believed him. "We just have one more to get, and we'll have the complete set."

Camden chuckled at her brothers being called "the set." Grandpa didn't mean it this way, but it was like we weren't all separate people sometimes.

"Good luck with that one, Grandpa. Cobb isn't coming to Kalamazoo," I assured him.

"Oh, your mother has tricks up her sleeve."

I shook my head before he'd finished talking. "Cobb has a clause in his contract that he can refuse a team." Smart fucker. I'd learned he'd had that added after I'd been traded here.

"It pays to be a baseball phenom, I guess." Camden gave me a toothy grin. If we weren't across from our grandpa, I would've given her a middle finger.

"All I'm saying," I emphasized for her benefit, "is that if Cobb ends up here, it'll be because he has no other choice."

We only stayed twenty more minutes, but then I had to get to the park. There was one more conversation that I needed to have.

Seeing how much older and frailer Grandpa had gotten made me realize how long it'd been since I'd seen him. It was sad to watch the once lively man from when I was growing up move so slowly now.

Madden was already at his locker when I got into the clubhouse, and there were only three other people there, and they all looked busy with their own shit. So I was able to go to Madden, where we likely wouldn't be overheard.

"What's up?" he asked as he scrolled his phone.

"That woman you were talking to yesterday… it looked like you were bothering her."

One corner of his mouth raised into a weird half-grin. "She wasn't bothered. She's just playing hard to get."

I shook my head, already feeling the burn of anger boiling in my chest. That shit pissed me off. Because guys used that as an excuse, and fuck me if I'd stand by and watch it. If I didn't want someone using it on Camden, then it wasn't going to fly on any woman in front of me.

"That's not how this works," I told him. "I talked to her in the parking lot. She wants you to leave her alone."

Now, he pushed to his feet and dropped his phone into his chair while puffing out his chest like he thought he was going to intimidate me. That wouldn't be happening. Had he not seen my brothers? That was who I'd grown up with.

"What'd you mean, you talked to her in the parking lot? You trying to fuck her?"

My jaw tensed. The woman might've been the most beautiful woman I'd ever seen but was I trying to fuck her? I didn't even know her name. Not to mention, I wasn't about to create any attachments here when I was leaving at the end of the season.

Though now he'd put the idea in my head… no. That would make me as bad as him. If I wasn't leaving though… I'd definitely want to spend time with her.

"No." My tone was short and clipped. "But I don't think she wants to be fucking you."

"Yeah, well, too late for that." His admission made me uneasy.

"Wait, wait, wait…" I waved my hand as I spoke. "So you already fucked her, and now she wants you to leave her alone." I chuckled, but it wasn't real. "That's not too impressive."

Madden's hand closed and opened, like he was trying to decide if he was going to hit me. If he had any brains at all, he wouldn't do it in the clubhouse. "Fuck off, Briggs. This is none of your business."

"I'm not going to stand by and watch you make a woman uncomfortable." And it had nothing to do with how fucking beautiful that woman was. "So, leave her alone, and we won't have to talk again."

"I think I'll have to ask her why she ran to you about this."

"She didn't," I snapped. "So learn that no means no. Don't bother her again."

Then I walked away knowing that he wasn't going to leave her alone and I wasn't going to let her, or any woman, be harassed by my teammate.

CHAPTER 4
EVERLY

Had I expected a man to be leaning against my car as I tried to leave for work?

I had not.

I sure as hell hadn't expect it to be Bryson Madden. As if he didn't have better things to do. I sure as hell did. Not to mention… why the hell does he know where I live. I almost never bring a guy to my apartment and I certainly hadn't him.

On instinct, I pushed my hand into my purse to pull out the small can of pepper spray that I always had in there and shove it into my back pocket. This was going to far even for him.

"Please tell me you're not really here," I said as

I passed by him to open my trunk and drop a bag in there.

One thing working with kids had taught me: Always have spare clothes close by.

"You can see me," he said. "Clearly, I'm here."

"I was hoping it was a nightmare that I could wake up from."

He snorted. Bryson was good-looking enough, and he had the cocky swagger of a professional athlete that I normally would've fallen all over myself for. He just didn't have the bandwidth to understand that I don't. Do. Relationships. It had been made clear to him, yet here we were.

"Baby, I'm not a nightmare. I'm a fucking dream."

"Right now, you're a wraith sucking my fucking will to live."

He narrowed his eyes. "A what?"

"A wraith." Then I rolled my eyes. "A nightmare demon. A scary mythological creature that feeds on people's fear. The only problem is, I don't fear you. I just want you to go away."

He chuckled, as if he thought I was being cute, and this was foreplay. "Listen." He stepped closer, so I stepped back. "I want to see you tonight."

I sighed and dropped my head back for a

minute. "Bryson, I know you're not stupid. What's going on here? I've made it abundantly clear that we won't be seeing each other again."

"I'm not used to being told *no*."

"Well, it's a big day for you, then."

Luckily, Bryson didn't strike me a as the kind of man who would react violently. Though you never could really tell, hence the pepper spray in my back pocket.

"Are you fucking Briggs?" he asked.

"Brooks? Are you out of your mind?" Brooks Briggs and I had worked at the camp together, but there had never been any friendly flirting—just friendliness. He had that same cocky nature about him that they all had, but for some reason, on Brooks, I didn't find it all that sexy. It also wasn't annoying on him.

"Not Brooks."

I furrowed my brows. "Camden? She's beautiful, but she doesn't have a penis."

He wet his bottom lip and shook his head. "I'm just saying that Briggs and I had a little chat. He wants me to leave you alone. Seems like maybe there's a reason for that."

I didn't know what he was talking about, but at this point, I'd take any help with him I could get.

"Uh, maybe he sees how fucking creepy you're being."

The way he hardened his eyes said he didn't believe me. But at least he walked away.

"This isn't over," he called over his shoulder when he got to his car.

Of course it wasn't. With him, I worried it never would be.

That was a very confusing way to start my morning.

At least he didn't make me late for camp.

Did I want to be puked on at eight in the morning by a kid who'd apparently eaten pure sugar for breakfast?

No, I did not. Yet it was still better than Bryson showing up at my apartment and waiting for me at my car like a fucking weirdo.

That kid was pissed that he had to go home until his stomach stopped revolting, but the rules were the rules. These kids were nine and ten years old. All they wanted to do was have fun and meet the professional players coming today.

Once I'd changed my clothes, I met all the other kids, said goodbye to their parents, and was leading them down to the baseball diamond the camp had set up. Since this place had been started by the owner of a major league team, let's just say the diamond reflected that.

It was better than the ones most of the kids played on with their teams.

When we turned the corner to the diamond, I came to a stop, causing the twenty kids behind me to as well.

There were four men on the field already, hitting balls and running after them. No one was supposed to be out here yet; however, four professional players were supposed to arrive soon. Maybe those guys were them, but it was my job as the adult to make sure my kids were safe.

"Wait here," I told them and my co-counselor, a sixteen-year-old girl named Robin.

The men could've been the pros there for the kids, or they could've been a group of weirdos. I didn't know. The batter was tall and muscular, with dark hair pushed back in a way that looked natural, though I doubted it was.

His smile could bring the devil himself to Earth. I had to shake that thought off, but it was incredibly difficult. This man was the most beautiful man I'd ever seen and also somewhat familiar. Like I'd seen him before, but I couldn't place where.

"You're kind of big to be a camper," I called out

to the man with the bat when I was within earshot, making four of them stop. Once I got closer, I recognized the pitcher and everything about me relaxed. That was Brooks Briggs. He'd been volunteering here long before I'd gotten this job. Which meant the other three had to be players, too.

"I thought I was only going to meet you in parking lots," the one with the bat called out. I narrowed my eyes.

He was Bryce's friend… or maybe not given his reaction about the guy. Either way, he was the guy in the parking lot that had wanted to make sure I was all right.

"Yeah," I said back. "I think that sounds worse than you probably meant it to."

"I heard it as soon as it came out of my mouth." He nodded in agreement.

Now that I knew the guys weren't weirdos trespassing on the camp, I waved the rest of my group over. The kids all started chattering excitedly.

This section was open to everyone at the camp in their age group. However, it was mostly boys who signed up. This year, there was one girl and I had to admit, I liked her moxie.

"I'm Everly," I told the four of them. "Nice to see you again, Brooks." He was, after all, the only one I actually knew, but the guy with the bat scowled and gave Brooks a questioning look. "And these"—I waved my hand around to indicate the group I had with me—"are my campers."

"Hi, everyone." Brooks stepped forward, which told me he was going to be the leader of this thing. "I'm Brooks Briggs. This"—he pointed to the one with the bat—"is my brother Urban Briggs and on this side is my other brother Silas Briggs. Lastly, we have Jenner Greene."

My stomach clenched. So my hero in the parking lot was a Briggs. Now that I had that information, I could've kicked myself for not realizing it. The three of them looked related. So much, in fact, that I should've guessed.

Wait… was the Briggs Bryson had been talking about this morning?

How big was the damn Briggs family?

"We know who you are!" an excited kid called out.

Glad they did because I didn't. Sports weren't exactly my thing. If they hadn't needed the introduction, I had.

Brooks came over to me and stopped once he was close enough that he wouldn't have to speak very loudly. "We were thinking of breaking the kids up into groups to cycle them through some things. We've got two hours with four groups, so maybe twenty minutes, and then we'll play a couple of rounds."

"That sounds great. Let me know what you need us to do, though, as I warned you last year, I'm not a sporty kind of gal."

He chuckled. "We're going to change that eventually."

I shook my head because I highly doubted it.

"My coordination when it comes to sports is lacking. I think it's better for all of us if I remain a spectator."

Brooks was unbelievably good-looking, but talking to him once had told me that I didn't want to sleep with him. He was the kind of guy a women fell for—like *really*, fully fell for.

And I wasn't into falling.

The guys broke up our group and took them to different parts of the field. With nothing to do, Robin and I sat on the second row of the bleachers to watch. If anyone got hurt, we had the first-aid kit. We also had the cooler of water, which the kids would run up to randomly for a bottle. Every little bit, we took a break so the kids could cool in the shade and hydrate. It was summer, after all.

On the last break before we moved onto something else, the brother Brooks had introduced as Urban stopped next to me under a tree where I had all the kids sitting.

"They have a lot of energy," he said, and at first, I wasn't sure he was talking to me.

"I wish I could bottle it," I told him. "Or get a hit off one of them or something."

He chuckled and then drained the rest of his water bottle.

"Anyone need the restroom?" I called out. Five raised their hand.

"I'll take them," Robin offered. Robin had her brown hair in a pixie cut which had to feel good in the summer but she had the features for it. She reminded me of an elf from a movie.

I'd worked here for four summers now and Robin was by far the most helpful teen counselor I'd ever had. Now this was day one and she might peter out, but for now, she was my favorite.

I stayed to watch over the rest of the kids while she did that. One of the boys threw himself onto the grass dramatically, making me laugh.

"Is it too hot out here for you, Landan?" I asked him.

He shot himself into an upright position. "No.

It's just hard being a baseball player." He shook his head, which made the actual players laugh.

When I looked back at Urban, it clicked where I'd seen him before. "Why'd you come out to me in the parking lot?" I asked, trying to keep my voice down. This probably wasn't the time or place but I wanted to know.

He turned to me slowly with his brows down. "What?"

"The parking lot at the department store on Saturday," I said more quietly. "You came out to find me right? Find us? Why? I didn't remember where I'd see you at first and then it clicked."

One brow raised high. "I play professional baseball, which means I'm on TV like six times a week. Maybe you've seen me there."

I shook my head and noticed that the other three guys had moved away and were in what looked like an enthusiastic conversation. Not intense, but they'd probably moved away because they were using words that ten-year-olds shouldn't hear.

"No," I told him honestly. "I don't watch sports. You came out and asked about Bryson. Why?"

He wet his bottom lip and took a breath like he was annoyed that I'd figured it out. "Yeah." A silence hung between us as I tried to decide whether I was going to ask him why he'd sought me out or if he'd talked to Bryson. "You looked uncomfortable."

"In the store?" I asked. He nodded. "I was. That man doesn't know how to stop." Though they could've been best friends and here I was on the verge of talking trash about that guy. Maybe not the best idea. "If he's your friend—"

"Teammate," he said, interrupting. "Not friends. I just got traded to the team last week."

Now it was my turn to furrow my brows. "Doesn't your family own the team?"

He nodded. "That's why I never wanted to be on it."

But he left it there, with me wanting to know the story behind that statement, as Brooks called for everyone to join him. They picked teams and played a little scrimmage; all the while, the pros gave the kids tips and pointers. Surprisingly these big strong professional athletes were gentle with the kids, tossing the ball like they were tossing a fragile egg. Robin and I cheered for both sides.

Too soon for the kids, it was time to head back for a snack. They packed up the equipment that we'd lugged down here. It was my turn to carry the equipment bag and Robin's turn to carry the cooler since we'd done the reverse on the way here.

Before I could swing the bag up onto my back, Urban was there taking it for me.

"You don't have to carry it," I told him.

"I don't mind," he said back, and I noticed that Silas took the cooler from Robin while Brooks and Jenner grabbed anything else that needed to be taken.

"Thanks."

We were only a few minutes into our hike back when I asked, "So your friend *was* bothering me on Saturday."

He shook his head. "Not my friend, remember?"

"Right." I swallowed hard. "Given that he's your teammate, I shouldn't have agreed to let you talk to him. It's my problem, not yours."

He furrowed his brows. "I don't give a shit that he's my teammate."

"Language!" one of the kids called out.

The other guys laughed, and Brooks said, "Yeah, language, Urban."

I snickered as he tried not to laugh. "I don't care that he's my teammate. I'm not going to stand around while a man makes a woman uncomfortable. It's not OK."

"So your mother raised you well, then?"

He shrugged. "I guess."

"Well, thanks." Though I wasn't going to mention that whatever he'd said to Bryson hadn't helped given that the dumbass showed up at my apartment—the place he wasn't even supposed to know about—just this morning. The reason I'd keep that to myself was that they were coworkers and I wasn't going to knowingly cause a problem between the two of them.

This was my problem. I'd have to deal with it.

"He's been bugging you for a while?" Urban asked bringing me out of my own thoughts.

"Since last year," I told him, unsure why I was. I guess if he tried to help me out, he deserved to know why. "We had a thing. I didn't want to have another. He's finding that hard to accept, and here we are."

We came to a stop outside of the mess hall. I told Robin to take the kids in, and I'd put away the equipment and then join her. They all ran off.

"You know, we really need an equipment shed by the ball field," I told him. "It makes sense. You should put in a good word to your parents or whoever." I bit back a smile. "Or maybe the four of you players could build us one."

It was only sort of a joke. It would make sense to have one down there so we wouldn't have to lug that big bag back and forth. Someone else should've already thought of that. Hell, I should've thought of it four years ago.

He smiled that devilishly beautiful smile. "I'll see what I can do."

When we walked over to where Silas, Brooks, and Jenner were putting everything away.

"Thanks for today," I told them. "The kids will be absolutely giddy the rest of the day. Probably insufferable."

"It's always fun," Brooks told me.

"Reminds me of when we were kids and baseball was just fun," Jenner added.

Silas furrowed his brows. Seeing the three brothers together reminded me just how much they resembled each other. Urban was the best-looking of the bunch, and they all had slight differences, but there wasn't a person on the planet who wouldn't know that they were related.

"Wait." Silas held his hand up. "Baseball used to be 'just fun' for you guys?"

That had them breaking out into loud laughter

at what I thought was probably an inside joke. I wished I could ask them to explain. But that wasn't really my place. Either way, their laughter was infectious making me laugh along with them.

"Anyway," I said once they'd calmed down. "They really will be talking about this the rest of the day. And then we start all over tomorrow."

Urban nudged my arm with his elbow. "Who comes tomorrow?"

"I don't know," I told him. "Camden puts that together."

"Oh, right." Urban snapped his fingers. "You know our sister."

The three of them groaned as Jenner shook his head.

"I like your sister," I told him. "She doesn't like baseball players, either."

"She likes us," Brooks countered.

I cocked my head to the side. "Does she?" Again, they laughed loudly.

"We've got to go," Brooks told them. After we said goodbye, I turned to walk away, and so did they.

Then I heard my name called out.

When I looked back, Urban was jogging over to me.

"Something wrong?" I asked.

He shook his head. "Nah. I wanted to see if you'd let me take you to dinner."

"You're asking me out?" My tone conveyed my confusion for sure, and I cocked my head to the side. Urban was a smoke show. There was no doubt of that but we'd literally spent two hours, not even together, and here he was asking me to dinner.

Something inside me said it was because he felt bad for me but that was probably my mother talking. It was true I'd met Bryson here at the camp but he didn't ask me out and we didn't discuss hooking up here.

"Yeah. Is that weird?"

After glancing around to make sure none of the kids had snuck out of the main building, I shrugged. "Maybe a little. We're at a kids' camp."

My answer should've been *no* immediately. But that devilish grin came out again and I could completely understand how he probably got tons of women to drop their panties for him. One flash of that smile had me forgetting that I wasn't going to hook up with any more baseball players.

It'd only been one in the four years I'd worked here but that was still biting me in the ass.

"I'm known for taking my shot."

For a reason that I didn't want to think about, the cockiness of the professional athlete didn't bother me with Urban. It was almost endearing, and maybe it was because he looked like he was a grown man who hadn't forgotten the little boy inside of him.

That made me sound insane even to myself but I didn't now what it was or why his question didn't immediately have me running for the hills.

"Sure. I'll have dinner with you tonight. You have a game?" I had no idea how any of this worked.

"I do. If you want to come to the game, we could go out right after."

Without meaning to, I scrunched up my nose.

He folded his arms over his chest and sighed. "Not a fan?" he asked.

"I already said that I'm not, but I did take the kids to a day game last year. It wasn't the worst." I nibbled on my bottom lip as I thought it over. "OK. I'll come to the game, and we can go eat after. Do I buy a ticket when I get there? How does this work?"

He snorted. "I'll tell Camden to work it out with you. You said you know her."

I nodded. "I love Camden."

He laughed again. "Everyone seems to."

Urban was about to turn away again, but before he did, I said, "I feel like I should warn you."

Now he raised an eyebrow. "That we're not going to have sex on the first date? It's not a problem for me." He said that as if he'd heard it before and surprisingly sounded sincere when he said it wasn't a problem for him. But me… I take a different approach.

Fighting the smile that broke out across my face was useless. "No. We can absolutely have sex if you want to. You're very attractive, and there are worse ways to spend the time. What I want to warn you is that I don't do relationships. At all. So it'd be just that. Sex."

He looked like I had just knocked the wind out of him. Yet his words seemed to contradict that. "You're speaking my language."

Now I had questions. Had he asked me out, knowing he wouldn't want a relationship with me? That was fine. I didn't want one with him, but now I felt the need to know what was going on in his head. Though I'd never met a guy that had a problem with no strings attached sex. I was sure they were out there but I'd never crossed paths with them.

"The game should hopefully be done at nine. Is that too late?" he asked.

"Not for me." I shook my head.

He wet his bottom lip. "I'll make sure Camden gets you where you need to be."

"See you after the game." I waved over my shoulder after I turned away.

Suddenly, my night promised to be much more interesting than I'd originally thought it'd be.

If I were being honest, I would've told him I didn't need the dinner because I didn't. We could've gone to his place—never to mine—and fucked like animals all night and I would've been satisfied.

But tonight... I wanted dinner first.

That should have been my first sign to run in the other direction, but there was something about Urban Briggs and tonight... I was going to find out what that was.

CHAPTER 5
URBAN

My brothers, Jenner, and I had ridden to the camp together. It had made sense, given that the four of us all had to be back on the field to get ready for our game tonight.

"What was that?" Jenner asked once Brooks had gotten us on the road.

He was talking to me, but I was confused. "What was what?"

He shook his head at me as if I were being purposefully dense, but I didn't know what he was talking about.

"You and Everly. You know her?"

"No." That much was true. "Madden was giving her a hard time at a store over the weekend, and I stepped in, but I don't know her."

Silas growled from the front seat. "That fucker's a good baseball player, but he's shit as a person." I didn't really know the guy, so I couldn't really disagree, especially given that all the information I had already led me to the same conclusion. "I saw Amity alone with him once. She was just updating travel documents, but I about lost my fucking mind. We weren't even together. It's not that I thought she'd do anything, but *him*…"

"Yeah, that'd piss me off, too," Brooks told him.

"We should all get dinner tonight after the game," Jenner offered up.

Jenner had always been like another Briggs brother. He had always been around since we were kids and he acted like one of us, anyway. He'd be the first to admit that he'd benefited from his position as an honorary Briggs as far as baseball was concerned. When our dad had started riding our asses, he'd ridden Jenner's too. The only difference was Jenner had gone home to a loving dad after that and we'd gone home to more baseball drills.

"Can't," I said first. "I have plans."

Silas turned to me with his brows slammed down. "Since when? You've only been in town a few days. Do you even know anyone else but us?"

I snorted. "You forget that I'm from here. Of

course, I know people. Doesn't matter that I haven't lived here in years."

"Maybe he and Dad are going to spend some quality time together," Brooks said in that shitily taunting voice he'd used even when we were kids.

"Fuck. Off." None of us would try doing that, but especially me. For whatever reason, I didn't get over shit as quickly as my brothers did. "I'm getting dinner with Everly."

"That was fast." Brooks looked at me in the mirror before focusing back on the road. Thank fuck we were almost back to the ballpark.

"You know how I work." Though honestly, that was a reputation that could've been applied to any of us or all of us.

Brooks pulled into the parking garage and the four of us got out. We still had time before we had to dress for batting practice. On the days that we would be at the camp, we'd get a pass on some of the exercises, but not any that would mean we'd get hurt.

Warm up improperly once and your entire career could be over.

"Urban," Brooks said, making me slow down for him to catch up. Jenner and Silas were fucking around with each other, pushing and trash-talking, on their way into the park like they'd done as kids. It was like they'd gotten older but also really hadn't.

"What's up?"

We began our walk in, though slower than the others had been. "Wanted to talk to you about Everly."

My stomach tightened. Something none of us brothers would do was fuck a woman another of us had. We were already brothers. No need to become closer that way. There was just something about it that we wouldn't be able to stand. Not because a woman can't have a past, but knowing your brother had been there… pass. Also, that could cause some unneeded drama.

"What about her?" I asked.

"Don't fuck her over."

I yanked the door open so we could step inside. "Didn't plan on it."

He scowled. "I know how you are. Fuck. It's no different than the rest of us, but she's a nice woman, and she works hard."

"You fuck her?" This wasn't the first time I'd asked one of my brothers this question. Probably wouldn't be the last.

Brooks grunted. "That's not what this is about. I've worked at the camp with her a few years now and there's just always been something…" He sighed. "Gut feeling that maybe she doesn't have it the easiest and doesn't need a baseball player fucking her over."

"Didn't plan on it." We turned down the hallway where the clubhouse was. "Fuck her? Yes. Fuck her over? No. Besides, she's the one who said she didn't need dinner first. She just wants it."

He chuckled. "I can see her saying that."

"How well do you know her?"

He shook his head as he said, "Not well at all. Just a few years of stuff like today."

"Good. Let's keep it that way." Then I yanked open the door to the clubhouse because this conversation was over.

Before Brooks had said something, I hadn't had this weird, protective feeling for Everly. Wait. Scratch that. I must have, given that I'd told Madden to leave her alone. Why would I do that if I hadn't felt a little protective of her in that store?

Convincing myself that I would've done that for any woman was easy. I would have. But Madden talking to her grinded my gears a little harder. It made no sense. I didn't know the woman, yet here we were.

As I got ready, I realized that there were some

things that I'd learned about Everly today just watching her at camp.

She clearly cared about the kids she was in charge of.

She was patient as hell with them but didn't sound like she was trying to be a disciplinarian.

The camp had started today, but she somehow already had those kids' respect. I knew enough about kids to realize that wasn't an easy task.

Everly was nice to all of us, even when she was keeping us at a distance.

I knew that much.

Tonight, I wanted to know more, though I didn't see the purpose since we were just getting together for tonight only.

I was just finishing up getting dressed in the clubhouse when Jenner nudged my shoulder with his. "How in the hell did you get Everly to go out with you in the two hours we were there this morning?"

I smiled widely. "Fucking talent. Mine's not all out on the field."

The guys chuckled with me. This was normal for us and probably for locker rooms in general, which was basically what a clubhouse is.

"Nah," I told them. "I just fucking asked. And

she's damn near perfect. She doesn't want a relationship, and neither do I." Which had surprised the hell out of me. I'd been taken aback when she said but thought I recovered rather quickly.

"Oh, fuck." Brooks was suddenly very serious. "You just called her *perfect*, which means you're definitely getting married."

"Fuck you." There was no malice in my words. None at all, but it was well known that I didn't intend to get married for a very long time—if ever. It wasn't worth it to me.

Yet for some reason, the image of Everly in a yard with a big house behind her, laughing with a couple of little kids that happened to look a lot like me flashed through my mind. Fuck that. No. We weren't doing that. There was no reason for that particular image to be there.

We ran through all of the shit we did before a game then came back to grab a bite to eat and get ready to warm up and play our game.

I did an excellent job keeping my head focused on what I was supposed to be doing. I was new to the team and still proving that I had a place here, even if I didn't want one. But if I fucked up here, it'd affect where I could go at the end of the season.

And I really didn't want to fuck up my chances of leaving.

Being in Kalamazoo, we took the field first and that was the first time I allowed myself to scan the area where I knew Camden would be sitting. She'd been there every game since I'd been back, sitting there with Amity, probably talking more than watching. Which meant Everly was likely to meet Amity as well.

Fuck. That might've been a little more familiar than I wanted her to get. She'd already known Camden and it sounded like they were friends so that didn't bother me. But Amity wasn't someone she'd come into contact with otherwise.

For a woman who said she despised baseball players, Camden sure did love the game. Only today, Everly was sitting there with them.

Everly sat next to Camden with dark sunglasses on. The sun would go down behind the side of the field soon enough but for now, they were on. She was laughing at something I assumed my sister or Amity said and the three of them were talking animatedly to the point that I wasn't sure if any of them were paying attention to the game.

My stomach clenched because she was what I'd

be doing after the game and fuck if I didn't wish that was now.

First, we had nine innings to play.

In the third inning, I was on second with a hefty leadoff. Their shortstop, Gutierrez, was just to my right, ready to rush the base if the need arose.

"I see your sister over there, Briggs," he said so only I would hear him. Trash talk was normal on the field, but since we were adults, it usually remained playful. Usually.

"Fuck off, Gutierrez." I kept my eye on the pitcher because I wasn't going to miss a chance to steal.

"She's looking good." He was just trying to get me riled up and it wasn't going to work. He wasn't the first to use Camden this way and wouldn't be the last.

"You know, there're three of her brothers on the team now. Four, if you count Jenner, which you should. You really want to stoke that fire?"

Again, we were professionals. We weren't going to have an all-out brawl on the field unless it had to do with the game. That didn't mean any one of us wouldn't have stepped up to protect our sister. Of course we would. And he'd regret it.

Luckily, there was a wild pitch that the catcher

missed, which gave me the opportunity to take third. Their catcher was fast, but I was faster. I took off, and between my lead and speed, I didn't even have to slide.

Since coming to Kalamazoo, that slump I'd been experiencing had thankfully disappeared.

In the end, we won the game… Actually, we kind of embarrassed them. The score wasn't even close, which meant that our clubhouse was full of energy once we all got down there. People were talking loudly, yelling even when it wasn't necessary. We were all around rowdy, but I was in a hurry. Winning this game had put us in first place. It was still early in the season, so anything could change, but for now, we were on top.

"In a hurry?" Jenner was trying not to smile. He knew damn well where I was going and exactly what I'd be doing. Chances were he was going to be doing the same thing, just with a different person.

I didn't answer him as I grabbed my wallet and keys then lifted a finger over my shoulder as I walked away.

Everly was right where I wanted her to be. Just down the hall from the clubhouse. She was standing there with Amity and Camden. Her caramel-colored hair was pulled up into a bun and she was wearing distressed jean shorts and a baggy top that was tucked into the front of those shorts. Her sandals were flat and her small purse was across her body the way Camden wore hers.

She wasn't dressed up, but my mouth watered anyway.

Everly was fucking beautiful. Anyone could see that, but there was something about her that I couldn't put my finger on that drew me to her. She didn't know I was watching and when the big smile appeared as she talked to my sister, it did something to me. A jelly kind of feeling filled my chest.

That wasn't something I was familiar with. That feeling.

I wanted Everly naked for sure. Seemed she wanted that too, but this other thing… I wasn't sure what it was and I wouldn't be mentioning it to anyone else.

"Good game, big brother." Camden reached up a hand for a high-five, which I gave her. She'd done it after games since she was like four years old.

"Thanks," I told her, then I focused on Everly, who was standing with her arms crossed under her breasts and the corners of her mouth turned up. "You ready to go?"

Camden groaned. "Be nice to her."

I wet my bottom lip. "Oh, I plan on being *really* nice to her."

Now my sister made a frustrated growl in her throat. "Don't be gross."

I chuckled, as did Everly before she told me she was ready to go.

Everly talked about the game until we were inside my car and I asked, "Have any cravings? Anywhere you want to eat?"

"Well…" She pulled at a string on her distressed shorts. "There's a food truck festival over in Tri Plaza. Some of those trucks are amazing."

Not exactly how I usually ate but I'd go wherever she wanted to tonight. "We can go there." I started the car up and pulled it out of its parking spot.

"We don't have to if you don't want to. I know it's probably not what you normally eat."

"It's fine with me." It was true we had to maintain nutrition, but that didn't mean we didn't deviate from it at all. Just not that often. However, my brother, Silas, stayed on the straight and narrow the most.

We made small talk, mostly about the camp, as I drove the six miles to the plaza.

Once there, we got out and headed to the first truck.

"For the festival, each truck has kind of made more of a tasting menu," she explained. "That way, you can get the gist of each place without your stomach exploding."

"That's smart." I doubted I'd eat most of it, but I was hungry.

"How about you hit these two trucks, and I'll hit these two?" She pointed to the other side of the area. "Then we can meet back at the table and we can share."

"Sounds good." I started to turn away then thought better of it. "Hang on a second."

Everly looked up at me with her big, green eyes that had flecks of gold in them. I pushed my hand into her hair and ran my thumb over her smooth cheek.

Everything inside of me was telling me to kiss her. I wanted to so badly, I could already taste her. The way her lips parted, I knew she wanted me to as well.

I lowered my lips to hers and at first, it was a chaste kiss. But then she pushed up onto her toes and I wrapped an arm around her waist. My tongue slid over hers and everything else around us disappeared. It was like we were the only two people in that plaza parking lot.

I would've left with her right then and there if I could have, but I'd said dinner, so we were having dinner.

After bringing that kiss to an end, I released her. Everly's cheeks were flushed pink and I didn't think it was embarrassment. Maybe that was what she looked like when she was turned on.

I'd find that out again later.

"OK… food," she said, sounding slightly breathless.

"Food." I kissed her again quickly before stepping back

Watching her walk away was time well spent.

Everly was on the shorter side—at least compared to me, though I was damn tall. Her legs were toned and looked so silky smooth that I could imagine… nope. Couldn't go there or I'd be standing in the middle of a food truck festival with a rock-hard cock.

Not ideal.

I went to get one plate from each place then turned to figure out where to sit, but Everly was already seated at a table for four. So I joined her. I'd brought food from the burger truck—which meant sliders, and the taco truck—which meant tiny street tacos. She'd gotten fries at the fry truck—though I couldn't believe they had an entire truck just for fries, and what looked like some kind of steak bites from the steak truck.

"This smells so good." She took another deep breath just to savor the aroma in the air.

"It does. Are you a picky eater?"

She snorted. "Not at all. I'll put just about anything in my mouth."

I chuckled low in my chest. That was meant for me. "That's really good to hear."

She shook her head. "You know, most people would be scandalized by that."

"I guess I'm not most people."

She watched me for at least thirty seconds before taking her first bite. It was from the steak truck and I think it was a garlic steak bite. She closed her eyes and sighed.

"That is so good," she told me. Then she switched gears. "OK. I need to know how in the hell you got the name Urban."

That wasn't the first time I'd been asked that question. "My dad. He wanted us all to be named after baseball players yet, somehow, he didn't name any of us after himself."

"Your dad's a baseball player too?" she asked, as if she'd had no idea and I believed her, but it wasn't often that someone didn't know who my dad was. I furrowed my brows. "Wait. Should I have already known that?"

I shook my head. "No. You don't need to have known that, but most people do, so it took me by surprise. You didn't google me before tonight?"

"Not a chance. Do you know the things I could probably find out about you on the internet? Pass."

Again, not the usual response.

"So, what about you?" I asked her. "You aren't into baseball and you don't like sports in general. What about your family?"

She set the fork down and looked at me seriously. "This isn't a date, Urban. You don't want to hear about my family. It's not a happy story."

With those words and the look on her face, I now desperately wanted to know.

CHAPTER 6
EVERLY

Urban had kissed me right there in the plaza, where anyone could've seen us. I didn't care, and I guess he didn't, either. I'd thought it'd have been more of an issue with him than me, given that newspapers didn't care what I did. I assumed some cared what he did since he was the "celebrity."

First, he'd kissed me, as if it had been the most natural thing in the world to do and then he'd asked about my family.

Why would he have asked about my family?

I'd spent my entire life being judged by what they did, and the last thing I wanted to do was tell Urban that I hadn't come from a family like his.

As I saw it, his family was clearly wealthy.

Camden had told me that all of her brothers were professional baseball players, but she'd never mentioned that their dad was that I could remember. But her mom's dad owned the team, and her mother would be the owner when he died. Camden's mother wanted Camden to take over when she couldn't anymore, and that wasn't something Camden was sure she wanted to do.

That was what I knew of her family.

Oh, and I'd met Brooks and Silas at the camp.

Now, that was it.

"What do you mean it's not a happy story?" he asked, and for the first time in a long time, something inside me urged me to tell him. That day in the department store with Bryson showed that Urban was protective—maybe not of me specifically, but of women in general, and I fell into that group.

But I wasn't going to. This wasn't a date, and he wasn't my boyfriend. He could ask anything else. With anything else, I was an open book.

"Ask something else," I told him, and I hated the pleading in my voice. "Ask anything else."

Urban paused like he was thinking about whether he should push a little hard or not and then nodded. Good thing too. Pushing me on my family was the quickest way to end the night. "What's with you and Madden?"

I rolled my eyes. "Of course that's what you'd ask." I swallowed hard and pushed the steak bites around my plate. "What other baseball player was named Urban? You didn't finish explaining about how your parents came up with the names." It wasn't important, but I was curious and it was something that would delay me answer the question he'd asked.

He regarded me seriously then took a breath. "Sure. So my dad wanted baseball names. My mom was fine with it. First came Brooks. He's named after Brooks Robinson. He played in the sixties era. Then came Silas. Now, Silas was named after our grandpa—"

"The one who owns the team?"

"That one. But there was also a player named Silas Simmons in the early nineteen hundreds."

"Did your grandpa play baseball?"

Urban shook his head. "He couldn't. Loves the game more than anyone I've ever met, but he got sick when he was a kid. His heart and lungs never fully recovered."

"That's really sad."

"It is," he agreed quietly. "So, then it came me,

and he decided to really go more obscure. There was a player in the nineteen twenties named Urbain Shockcor. People called him 'Urban Shocker.'"

I giggled. "That is an amazing name. Urban Shocker."

"Tell that to a kid in middle school named Urban."

I covered my mouth to keep from laughing more. Middle school would've been hard with that name.

"Wait. Is your middle name Shocker?" Because, in my imagination, that would've been epic, though awful, as a kid.

"No." He chuckled. "My middle name is Conrad. Actually, all of our middle names are Conrad, after my dad." He lifted the water bottle to his mouth to take a drink.

"Even Camden's?"

When he snorted, his cheeks puffed out a little, like he was trying not to spray the water all over me.

"Not Camden. But I will be calling her 'Camden Conrad' from now on."

I cringed. "Please don't. She'll hate me." I wasn't totally sure she would, but Camden and I were friendly from camp, and I didn't want it to be awkward.

"So they made fun of your name in middle school?" That was where we'd left off.

He shrugged. "I never minded, though. Then Cobb from Ty Cobb and Camden."

"Why didn't they name Camden something baseball-related?"

He stopped the fork with a piece of steak on it that had been headed to his mouth. "They did. Camden Yards. Famous baseball field?"

"Sorry." I shrugged. I'd never heard of it that I remembered.

He furrowed his brows as if my not knowing Camden Yards was impossible. "So… Madden."

I rolled my eyes because I'd hoped he had forgotten all about it. "I met him at camp last year. We hooked up once, and apparently, it was life-changing for him."

"But not for you?"

"Definitely not for me. Anyway, he pokes his head up every once in a while, trying to get me to go out with him. I've told him that I don't date and that I don't do relationships, but he doesn't seem to get it. Do baseball players get concussions?"

His brows pinched together. "Sometimes."

"Maybe he's had one too many because he just is not getting it."

Urban's loud laugh forced me to smile. This conversation was so weird. Most guys didn't want to know about anything you did in the past, even if you were only together for one night. Urban… wanted to know about me, and it was… unsettling.

Possibly in the best way I could imagine.

No. I had to kick those thoughts aside. I couldn't get wrapped up in this guy. Or any guy.

"You don't date," he said. "I don't date much, either. Haven't for a while, but this feels an awful lot like a date."

I couldn't argue with him there but I also wouldn't agree with him.

I quickly wet my lips and looked up at him with big, innocent eyes. "I just wanted to have energy for later."

Urban put his fork down, folded his big hands in front of him, and rubbed them a little, like people would if they were thinking about how to say something. "I'm not expecting anything, Everly. I asked you out because I wanted to," he told me. "We can just have this food, and I'll take you home if you've changed your mind."

Sex had been implied. Scratch that. *I'd* implied we'd be having sex and men didn't usually pass on that. I didn't mean just with me. It was a general thing.

Urban wasn't wrong, though. My other one-night stands, though there hadn't been *that* many, didn't go like this. Dinner didn't come first. Usually, I found someone attractive, made a move—or he did—and then we got naked.

I absolutely did not want to think about why I'd decided to get dinner with him first. It couldn't be because I liked him.

I mean… of course, I liked him; otherwise, I wouldn't be doing this with him tonight. The question remained: Why had I wanted dinner first? Sure, I did need energy for later, but I could've gotten that on my own.

Maybe I was fun drunk from the game. Amity, Camden, and I had more fun than I thought a baseball game would ever be.

There was something about Urban that I liked beyond what we were going to do tonight, and I seriously hoped we could be friends tomorrow.

Scratch that. I'd never been to this point with a one-night stand in my life. I'd never wanted dinner first. Every other time, we'd both been seeking a result. Sometimes, that result had been the release I'd wanted, and sometimes, it'd been Bryson.

Then I realized that I should've been looking for a man who would say he wouldn't care if we didn't have sex all along. Not for a relationship, but I could see Urban being someone I could be friends with and have sex with.

"Thanks for the offer," I told him. "I guess we'll see where the night goes."

He sat back and started eating again. "So why no relationships?"

"You really want to know?" I asked and he nodded. "I think you'd call it the *three strikes and you're out* rule. I've had a few. They went bad and I'm tired of starting over."

He furrowed his brows. "Isn't that kind of a jaded view for someone…" That was when he likely realized he didn't know how old I was. Clearly, he could see that I was an adult, but was I twenty or forty?

"Twenty-four. And no. I've had three serious relationships and got burned every single time. I don't want to do it again. Probably ever, given that I grew up in a house that didn't exactly model the healthiest relationships."

"Well, now I want to know even more."

I snorted. "We'll see. Maybe if we stay friends after tonight."

Once again, Urban had a look on his face that I wanted to ask about or, hell, crawl inside of, but I wouldn't do either. One beautiful man after another had burned me, and now, my heart was fireproof.

My heart was so well protected that the feelings peeking up about Urban surprised even me.

The two of us continued talking until we were both finished eating. He took the trash to the bin then led me back out to his car. He didn't touch me in any way, but he walked closely, and I kind of wanted to take his hand in mine. I'd never do it. Too *relationshipy*.

"Did you leave your car at the ballpark? I probably should've asked before we left," he said when we were in his car.

I snickered. "No. Camden offered to pick me up so I wouldn't have to worry about it."

"Excellent." He took a deep breath then blew it out. "So… you're place or mine?"

It was corny but to the point. "Well, I don't know. Who is closer?" What the hell was I thinking? The automatic answer should've been his. Not my apartment. I never brought anyone there but for some unexplainable reason, I trusted Urban enough to not worry about him knowing where I lived.

Clearly, they could find out anyway given Bryson showing up there without an invitation.

Urban told me where his apartment was and I groaned. Mine was much closer so I told him where I lived. He knew roughly where it was, and then I gave turn-by-turn directions to get him to the right building.

As we walked into my building and up the stairs, I began to wonder why in the hell I was doing this. Bringing Urban to my apartment wasn't normal for me but deep down, I didn't think I had to worry about my safety with him.

Maybe it was because of how he'd acted about Bryson. Maybe it was just the vibe he gave off.

Whatever it was, I felt safe with Urban. Safe having him in my house.

The only thing threatening my safety right now was the thoughts I'd been having about him.

I flipped the switch right inside the door so that we weren't in complete darkness. He shut the door behind us.

Right then, I wanted this to start but also didn't.

Don't get me wrong. I wanted to have sex with him, but I also wanted to continue the night as it had been. Talking to him was easy and I didn't find talking to men easy too often.

Hormones won out.

Urban pushed his fingers into my hair and cupped my cheek. He leaned down quickly, pressing his lips to mine.

That was when any battle waging inside me was gone. I wanted this. Wanted him.

His soft lips moved against mine. He trailed his tongue across my mouth so that my lips would part then he pushed his tongue inside and honestly, it was all gentler than it should've been, given what we were to each other.

Not friends, but a one-night stand, though we'd see each other again at camp eventually.

Gentle, like I was something special, wasn't something I could stand from him. It brought up potential and I didn't want to have potential with anyone at this point.

That was when I acted. I pushed against him harder, kissed him more demandingly, and pulled at his shirt.

Urban took the hint. He ran his hands down my sides until they cupped my ass, then he lifted. I wrapped my legs around his waist and my arms around his shoulders as his tongue stroked mine.

He pulled away and asked, "Bedroom?" He sounded slightly winded, but not in a way that made me think that I weighed too much for him to hold.

"On the left." I, on the other hand, sounded like I was on the verge of drowning.

Urban's mouth claimed mine again as he walked us to the bedroom.

Once inside, he dropped me onto the bed then pulled his shirt over his head. That shirt had looked good on him, but off of him was even better.

The heavily-muscled body builder had never been my type. Urban, however… was exactly my type. His chest and abdomen were hard with muscle that I assumed he'd gotten from swinging his bat, though he likely worked out quite a lot, given his job.

While there was some definition, it wasn't too much. At least, not for me. He was covered in lean muscle everywhere I could see. Just… strong.

"Come here." He wiggled his fingers. I scurried up so that he could pull my shirt over my head.

His gaze heated, set afire by the desire he must've been feeling. Or maybe it was mine. He kissed down my neck to the swell of my breast as his hands worked on the clasp on my bra around my back. Once it was loose, my breasts sprang free and his mouth took advantage.

I curled my hands tightly into his hair when he licked my nipple.

There was so much going on inside of me that I didn't think I'd be able to separate any of the feelings racing around. Ignoring them and focusing on the pleasure was the best I could do. Every single touch of his brought me closer to the edge.

Urban pulled away, leaving me half-naked so that he could flick the button on his pants and then push them down.

Now his cock sprang free and my stomach dropped like I was on the first big hill of a roller coaster.

He was long—but not too long. Thick—but not too thick.

With Urban, it was like a sculptor had asked me what the perfect man looked like to me, and then Urban appeared.

For a moment, I worried that I was too caught up in this already, but I couldn't be bothered with that.

Right now, he was all I wanted.

As if we knew what the other wanted without having to say it, I slid myself to the edge of the bed where I was almost at waist level with him. He threaded his hand back into my hair and pulled me closer to his cock. I wet my lips before taking it in my mouth. He groaned as I stroked my tongue over his length on my first pass.

"Fuck, Everly. Your mouth feels like silk."

A shiver of satisfaction raced through me. One of my favorite things was when a man lost control because of me. Because of that, I moved quicker. Faster. Used more pressure. Cupped his balls in my hand and used that to my advantage. I pushed myself so far down him that I gagged.

Urban made a strangled noise in his throat right before he nudged me away.

"You better stop," he said, sounding like he'd just run the bases. "On your back."

I hurried to where he wanted me. Urban let out a deep breath then undid the button on my shorts and pulled them down my legs with the panties still inside.

"Jesus," he muttered. "You're so fucking beautiful."

Except… he wasn't looking where I thought he would be when he said that. He was looking me in the eye.

This was too much. I didn't want him saying sweet things to me whether I was naked or clothed. That wasn't what we were here to do.

To get his attention elsewhere, I trailed my fingers up the inside of my thigh and over the area between my legs before rubbing a circle over my clit. His jaw tightened, then he gently slapped my hand away.

"That's my job." Urban dropped to his knees and yanked me to the edge of the bed. Then he pushed my knees as far apart as they would comfortably go.

He wet his lips quickly then ran his tongue over my clit. My muscles clenched, and my knees threatened to snap shut, but his big hands kept them open. Urban's talents weren't only on the field, apparently.

Urban played me like an instrument with which he was already well acquainted. As I got used to him between my legs, he released one knee and pushed a finger into me all while licking and sucking at my clit.

Dear hell, he was going to make me cum in record time.

As expected, the pressure built and I want to release while at the same time didn't want this to end. But ultimately, I didn't have a choice.

My orgasm ran over me in massive waves of

pleasure. I clenched at the blanket on my bed just to hold on for the ride.

That was intense.

Once the wave subsided, Urban pulled back and ran his hand over his mouth before waving it at me. "Roll over."

"Condom," I rasped out. "Top drawer." I assumed he'd know I meant my dresser.

"I have some."

"Top drawer," I repeated. One thing I always did was use my own protection. I wasn't about to leave my safety up to some guy I'd just met.

Though to be fair, I'd done that in relationships, too.

As if he understood, Urban went to the dresser. The drawer slid open then closed, a small tearing filled the room, then he was back behind me. I could feel his presence without looking.

While I was on my hands and knees, Urban pushed into me slowly, but in one thrust. I was more than ready for him, but he filled me to my max. Any more and it would've been too much.

Urban moved slowly, showing that he understood that from this angle, he was going to reach deeper and he'd be careful not to hurt me.

Then he moved faster several times before

pulling out. "On your back," he said and I was more than happy to give my wrists a break.

He was right back inside me, this time moving quicker and pushing me toward another release. Everything around me was Urban. The sound of his breaths coming faster. The sound he made when I dug my nails into his hard shoulders when he hit exactly the right spot. Once a second orgasm hit and subsided, he pushed into me three more times and groaned.

He'd found his release.

Urban lay on top of me with his head against my chest for so long that I worried he'd fall asleep. Just when I was about to say something, he lifted his head.

"I'll be right back." He kissed me deeply before heading to my bathroom.

That had been... phenomenal. How in the hell had he known exactly what I'd needed?

I didn't want to consider that, so I hopped up and grabbed a robe so I wouldn't be naked when he got back.

He did a double take when he entered my bedroom again. At first, he looked confused and then understanding came over him. I'd sort of gotten dressed so that meant he should too. He grabbed his clothes off the floor but watched me with a heavy gaze as he got dressed.

"So, I—"

"That was fun," I told him trying to sound like we'd just gone bowling and it was the most fun I'd ever had. Chipper and cheery even though I was wrought with confusion.

One corner of his mouth turned up. "Fun," he said flatly.

"Yeah. Uh… Maybe we could do it again some time."

His gaze narrowed on me. "Sure."

"You have a game tomorrow, right?" I asked. He nodded. "I don't want to keep you too late, then." Which was my way of saying *don't let the door hit you on the way out*. My stomach dropped and tightened when I said it and my throat started to burn. I didn't like these signs. They were symptoms that told me that my words and feelings weren't exactly aligning.

He really needed to go.

"Yeah." The muscle on his jaw bulged then released as he tightened and relaxed it. "Wouldn't want that, would we?" He got all of his things together then paused at the door. "We travel to a game tomorrow." Though he didn't need to tell me that. "I'll talk call you… or text."

"Sure."

Usually, when a guy said that, he wasn't going to do either and that was fine. Besides, it occurred to me that I never gave him my phone number nor did I have his. Probably for the best.

Right now, I needed some space from Urban Briggs because what we'd just done hadn't been like it had been with anyone else. That wasn't possible, right? Sex was just sex.

No reason to get attached.

So why was I already feeling attached to Urban?

CHAPTER 7
URBAN

*E*verly hadn't been wrong when she'd said last night had been fun.

Of course, it was fun, but fuck me if there wasn't a connection between the two of us. Since I was only staying in Michigan until the end of the season, I couldn't get attached to her or anyone else. Connection or not, I couldn't do a fucking thing about it.

Still, I couldn't dwell on it because I had to pack my bag and get my ass to the field. We had a flight and it was early so that we could get ready for our game that night. We were just playing in Minnesota, so it wasn't far and it wouldn't be for long.

It wasn't until we were on the plane that Silas

dropped into the seat beside me and Brooks in the one across the aisle. The plane that the team owned only had two seats on each side of the aisle and they were roomy enough for us not to feel cramped. There were a lot of big guys on the team. Flying commercial would've been a headache.

"What'd you do last night?" Silas asked as he tried not to grin like a fucking idiot.

"Probably the same thing you did," I told him as I locked my gaze with his. "What'd you do last night, Silas? I'd appreciate some details."

"Uh, fuck off," he said without any contempt behind it. "You might've been doing the same thing, but it's not the fucking same. I love Amity. She's it for me. Can you say the same thing?"

Of course I fucking couldn't. But after talking to Everly and being with her last night, I was beginning to wish that I could. Even if something could happen between us, I couldn't let it. I was determined to leave in a few months either way and wouldn't uproot anyone's life that way.

Not that I wanted to fall in love with her and sure as hell hadn't in the one night we'd spent together, but this gnawing in my chest made me wish that all of that was possible.

It was fucking stupid.

"Anyway…" Brooks cut in. "You didn't do anything that's going to make camp on Friday awkward, right?"

"Course not. I've never left anyone unsatisfied." Then I thought about what he said. "That's right. We're gone for Wednesday camp."

"Sure are, little buddy." Silas chuckled. "And they may not have been unsatisfied but there have been some that were left psycho."

I groaned. "Don't remind me. Breelyn was crazy good in bed, but it wasn't fucking worth it." She was the reason that I'd kept things casual since then. After her, I knew that it'd have to be a special thing to get me to consider settling down in anyway. Luckily, me leaving at the end of the season would keep that from happening.

We'd gone out a few times when suddenly I'd found her living in my apartment in Florida when I'd first moved there. Originally, I'd thought it was weird that she had always been there when I was away. I hadn't even given her a key. She'd made one herself. Anyway, then her shit was everywhere and it had taken me forever to get her to understand that we weren't that serious.

What a fucking nightmare.

"Anyway…" I wanted to change the subject. I

didn't normally tell my brothers—or anyone—what I did with a woman; I especially didn't want to tell them about what I'd done with Everly.

Or how she'd basically kicked me out when we were done.

"Outside of the normal reason," I began, "did Mom tell either of you why she got me traded?"

"She didn't get you traded," Brooks said immediately. "That's just part of the game."

"You know what I mean. Why now? It was a weird time. I wasn't on a hot streak—"

"A slump, more like it," Silas added.

I sighed. "Yeah. five games. I was really worried I couldn't play anymore," I told him sarcastically. "Seriously. Why now? Gramps said we just need Cobb and I told him that's not gonna happen."

Brooks narrowed his eyes and cocked his head. "Have you ever known Mom to not get what she wanted?"

No, I did not. "He doesn't want to be here. Even if they somehow got him here, too bad, I'm gone at the end of the season so there goes the plan to have the four of us on the same team."

Silas coughed then turned so he was facing both me and Brooks. "Look. None of us wanted to be here because of Dad, but now that I've been here a while… I don't really want to go anywhere else."

"That's because of Amity," I countered.

He shook his head. "I'd have to get her to come with me if I wanted to be on another team. Right now, my contract will keep me here for a while because Mom's not going to easily trade any of us and we all know it."

That was true. Once Mom got us here, she wouldn't let us go without a fight. "I'll take a pay cut and my contract is up at the end of the season."

Was that the smartest way to handle my career? No, probably not but I wanted out more than I wanted money. If I was honest, the Briggs family had more than they needed without the salaries. Too much almost.

"But now that I'm here," he continued, "I don't really want to leave. This team is good. Like, really fucking good. Mom knows what she's doing. I only have to deal with Dad sporadically, and we're all used to that." He sighed. "And as much as I might not want to admit it, I like playing with you guys again. Better than playing against you."

That was the selling point. "I can see that." Yet it still didn't convince me that it was the only reason I was here. "But why now?"

Brooks leaned over the aisle more, like he was about to tell us where his diary was hidden. "She doesn't think Grandpa has much longer left. His dream was to have us all playing on his team, so she's trying to give him that before it's too late."

When I'd gone to see him, he'd been moving slowly and the oxygen tank was there but he seemed fine. Looks could be deceiving though. No one would've guessed he had a life long heart and lung issue.

Fuck.

"Grandpa's dying?" This would be the first I'd heard of that.

"Not specifically, but he was older when he had Mom, so he's in his eighties. How much time could he have left?"

Yeah. That, I could see.

"Well, Cobb isn't ever going to do it," I said. "It'd take something huge to get him here and it'd have to be more than money." Cobb and I had talked about this after Silas had been traded to the Knights. My little brother was adamant he wasn't going to be on the Knights anytime in the near future. And right now, he had the clout to do it. That fucker was on his way to a Cy Young award this year. He was only twenty-three fucking years old.

"You know this for sure?" Brooks asked.

I nodded. "We talked. He doesn't want to be here."

"You know a couple of months ago, Grandpa told me about when he started dating Grandma." It sounded like Brooks was about to tell a story. "Grandma was dirt poor. The oldest of fourteen kids and the most beautiful woman he'd ever seen. Told me that I shouldn't settle for anyone whom I didn't think hung the moon. Anyway, she didn't want to get married."

I furrowed my brows. "Why not?" I mean, I didn't necessarily think I'd get married, but back then, it had practically been a damn given.

"She was dirt poor," he said slowly. "And the oldest of fourteen kids. She didn't want that life if she ever got out of it."

"Then Gramps came around with all of his money," Silas added. Because Grandpa had come from a rich family already. Then he'd made more money.

"Yeah, but she still didn't want to get married," Brooks said. "It's also why Mom's an only child.

So my grandma didn't want to get married yet was convinced to. I couldn't help wondering what had changed her mind. Did that mean other people who happened to be anti-relationship could have their minds changed? Nah. I had to push that out of my mind. I couldn't have a relationship with Everly, It was one night. Why the fuck was I wondering if her mind could be changed. I was leaving at the end of the year.

Everly was probably going to change her mind on relationships. Eventually she'd find someone she wanted that with. It just wouldn't be me and I told myself I was fine with it. I barely knew the woman and my time in Kalamazoo had an expiration date.

It wasn't until that night, after the game, that I realized I didn't even have Everly's phone number. How in the fuck could I call or text her if I didn't have her number?

The answer was, I couldn't. But I knew someone who probably had it.

"What can I do you for, brother?" Camden answered her phone. Normally, I would've sent a text, but this might require some sweet talking.

"I need Everly's phone number?" There was no reason to beat around the bush.

Camden snickered on the other end of the phone. "You didn't ask her for her phone number?"

"*Camden*," I warned.

"Hang on." She was still laughing and I could hear her doing something in the background, so she hadn't put me on hold. After what seemed like forever, she came back and said, "I just sent it to you." The ding sounded in my ear.

"Thank you," I told her. "I appreciate it."

"Well, she said you could have it."

"What?"

"I sent her a text," she explained. "Did you think I'd just give you her number without asking her first? Sorry, no. Sisters before misters. Even when it comes to brothers."

Well, at least Everly wanted me to reach out to her, I suppose. "Thanks." The word came out clipped, but I wasn't sure why. Camden had just done me a favor, and I should appreciate that.

"I get that you're not used to be told *no*, Urban, but I like Everly and I'm not going to do something like that without asking her." She sighed. "You know that Madden doesn't leave her alone, right?"

I gripped the phone tightly in my hand to the point that it threatened to crumble. "Yeah. I know. What do you know about that?"

"Uh… if she hasn't told you, I can't."

"Camden," I barked. "She's told me. I want to

know what you know about the situation."

"Probably just what you do and I only know because I was there when he was harassing her once right before camp ended last year."

"Why was he there?" I snapped. "The baseball clinics don't go that late. It'd fuck with the end of the season or post season if we made it that far."

"I know that and you know that, but Madden would show up unexpectedly from time to time. Like the other morning. At the game yesterday, she mentioned that he was waiting outside by her car when she went to leave for work."

"She didn't mention it to me." Anger flared in my chest and Madden was about to get a more severe talking to. After I cleared it with Everly. The last thing I wanted her to do was think that I was stepping in to play caveman, even if that was exactly what I wanted to do.

She wasn't mine. I didn't necessarily have the right to interfere beyond the fact that a teammate was harassing a woman.

"You stay away from him," I told her more gently so she'd know that I wasn't trying to boss her around.

Camden choked a little. "Brother. I stay away from *all* of them. I only go around you and the guys because you're blood-related. I hate ballplayers, remember?"

I did remember and none of us could ever figure out exactly why. Camden wasn't about to tell us but I'd bet her best friend Harlowe knew.

Sure, she'd told us some reasons, but I'd always had the sneaking suspicion that there was more to it. If Everly and I stayed friends as she'd suggested when we'd been at the food truck festival, maybe she'd get to the bottom of it for me.

Fuck... Friends... I suddenly hated that word.

"Yeah. I remember," I said, snapping back to the conversation at hand.

"All right, well, I have to go. Call Everly since that's the only reason you called me."

I put my hand to my chest and with fake outrage and said, "I'm crushed. You don't think I'd call my favorite sister just to hear her speak?"

I could practically hear her eyes rolling through the phone. "I'm your only sister."

"Just because you don't have competition doesn't mean you wouldn't be my favorite if you did."

She chuckled. We'd had this very conversation before. "Goodbye, Urban. Good luck with your game tomorrow."

I groaned. She knew she wasn't supposed to wish any of us good luck.

We all had our own superstitions, but that one was universal. Tell us to have a good game, sure. But never say *good luck*.

After ending my call with Camden, I took a minute before calling Everly. Then it hit me. She knew that Camden had given me her number since my sister had asked before doing it. If I waited too long, that would send a message.

So I brought up the Facetime app and hit the contact that my sister had shared.

On the second ring, Everly's face filled the screen.

"Hey," she said with a smile. At least she was happy to hear from me. That was good, I supposed. Her hair was down around her and she wasn't wearing any makeup. There wasn't a huge time difference between where I was and where she was but I'd guess she was already in her pajamas. "How was your game today?"

"It was good. We won. I hit two singles and a triple."

She scrunched up her eyebrows in the most adorable way. "Is that good?"

My loud laughter filled the room. "We're going to have to work on your baseball knowledge."

"Well…" She fell back onto her couch and held the phone where I imagined her knees would be if she'd pulled them up in front of her. "Yesterday was my second game, and I have to say, it's better without twenty ten-year-olds hopped up on too much sugar to watch over."

"I can see where that could be distracting."

She puffed up her cheeks then blew the air out like she was tired just thinking about the game she'd taken the kids to. "Last year when I brought the kids, I didn't have time to appreciate just how much I like baseball pants."

"I've heard that some women are fans." I ran my tongue over my bottom lip. "Did you learn anything about the game?"

"I did not. Or rather, not much. Camden tried to explain it, but it just doesn't make sense to me. There are so many rules."

"There aren't *that* many." My tone was defensive, but it was all for show.

She rolled her eyes. "Says the person who's been playing the game his whole life. It'd be like me throwing you into my high school English Lit class and having you teach the Brontës."

I cocked my head to the side. This was going to be fun. "You don't think I've read Brontë?"

She shrugged. "I don't know if you have or not, but reading it and teaching it are two very different things."

That, I'd give her. "High schoolers, huh?" I'd known she was a teacher, but not what grade she taught. High schoolers could be assholes and suddenly, I felt remorseful for any shit I'd ever given one of my teachers.

"Yeah. It's my favorite age group. They're funny, trying to be adults, but not quite there yet. They also can on my nerves."

"How so?"

"Two weeks before the end of the year, a kid had his phone out during a test and I'd already told him to put it away twice. Apparently, he was having trouble with his girlfriend and that was more important than what I had for them that day."

"Of course it was."

"What do you mean?"

I lay back against the headboard of the hotel bed to get more comfortable. "In high school, the most terrifying thing is thinking your girlfriend is pissed at you."

"Why's that?"

"Uh…" I scratched at the back of my head. "Well, if you really love her, you're afraid of losing her."

Everly bit back a smile when I wanted her to let it loose. Seeing her with a real smile… She was beautiful any way she looked, but that… It brightened up her face. "There seems like there's a story there."

I sighed. This wasn't going to make men look any better. "Also, if you're having sex with her, the idea of that going away and you being stuck with just your hand again is literally the end of the world."

Everly slapped a hand over her face as she let out a loud laugh. "I hadn't thought of that and honestly, I shouldn't think of that all when it comes to my kids."

"True. So what happened with the kid and the phone?"

"Oh, I was walking around the room, making sure they were all working on the test. The kid next to him saw me coming and told him that if he didn't put his phone away, Miss Rose was going to turn him into a hashtag."

"What the fuck does that mean?"

"I have no idea." She shrugged. "I'm not that

much older than them, so I probably should know but no idea. At least he put his phone away."

Given the time, I had to get off the phone, but it was the last thing that I wanted to do right then. Still, I had to get to bed because we were the visiting team, which meant all of our shit happened earlier than the home teams.

"We're missing camp tomorrow, so what do you do?" I asked her as my way of stalling the inevitable.

She shrugged. "Sometimes, the high school or college teams fill in when you're gone. Or we will take them on a field trip for that day which we aren't doing tomorrow. So, I guess I'm not sure what we're doing and I'll find out in the morning but your sister always has something to replace you."

"Ouch." I chuckled. "So easily replaced?"

She bit into her bottom lip and shook her head. "I promise, nothing excites the ten year olds more than having the pros there."

If I hadn't grown up with a pro ball player of a dad which meant other pro ball players were around a lot, I would've been like that. Seeing the guys actually doing what I wanted to one day would made my life.

Somehow, I retroactively was jealous of the other kids I'd grown up feeling that. I'd never had the chance. Then I sighed.

"I have to go," I told her quietly.

"No problem." But she took a breath and looked off of me before coming back. "Why did you want my number? Why did you want to call?"

This was the time for me to be honest with her. "Because I'd like to see you again when we get back. If you're into it."

She gave me an innocent smile. "I really think I'm too good in bed. One time with me and these professional baseball players are hooked."

At the same time, my stomach clenched because I knew she was talking about Madden as well, but I didn't know who else and also couldn't deny it.

"Well?" I asked. "And for the record, I didn't mean specifically for sex."

For a split second, she was unsure. I could see it in her eyes. But then she nodded and said, "Yeah. We can get together. Just let me know when you're back."

Oh, I'd be calling her tomorrow after the game again, but a couple of days after that, I'd absolutely let her know that I was home.

CHAPTER 8
EVERLY

$\mathcal{U}$rban called me every single day that he was gone, which I both loved and looked forward to as well as feared.

I was starting to expect the call and that was the first sign of danger as far as feelings went. Since I didn't do relationships, I shouldn't have done feelings, either. And this was starting to feel like feelings, yet I didn't want to run from it just yet. There'd be a point at which I did, but it wasn't now.

"So?" Jade asked as we were setting up her art room at camp. It was Friday and she taught a couple of classes here on Friday.

"So, what?"

She stopped and gave me the look. The one that said she thought I was being purposely thick. That I was intentionally not understanding what she was talking about, but that wasn't the case.

I just didn't know because she hadn't explained herself yet.

"You know what I'm talking about." Jade had her blonde hair wrapped up in a neat bun and while she was dressed for camp, it all looked elegant on her. She was taller than me, tall enough to be a model, and since she'd come from money, though she didn't act like it, she sure looked like it, even when she was dressed down.

"Jade." I put the last can of brushes on the long table. "I really don't know what you're talking about because you haven't told me."

She sighed and leaned against the desk in the corner that she almost never used. "It's been four days and you haven't told me about your night with Urban. That usually means… Wait. I don't know what that usually means because we share every- thing. Good or bad."

Jade was right. I hadn't told her about that night yet. "You went to see your parents. I didn't talk to you on Tuesday or Wednesday because believe it or not, we don't actually talk every single day. And yesterday, we were busy planning today."

"OK. But now we have some time. The kids

aren't here yet. You could tell me now. Was it awful? Was Madden not a fluke? Are all baseball players bad at sex?"

I snickered. She really wanted the information. "I can confirm that not all baseball players are bad at sex. Madden might not even be bad. Maybe we just didn't have the chemistry."

"Yeah, true. But what about Urban? Also, how the hell did he get that name? Do you know?" Talking to Jade was sometimes like being interrogated by the local police. All she was missing was the intense light right in my face, blinding me so that I'd spill my guts.

"Well, do you want to know about what happened between us or about his name? Because we don't have time for both."

"The sex, of course. You can tell me about his name another time."

"It was good. Fantastic, actually, and then I told him it was fun and we parted ways."

Her face dropped. "Is that really all you're going to tell me?"

"Do you want positions? Length? Girth? I'd draw you a picture if I had any talent," I said dryly. She snickered as I snapped my fingers. "Wait. You could draw it. I'll describe everything and you draw it like you're doing a police sketch."

Now she was full belly-laughing. "I don't suppose that's necessary, but you know it's been a while for me. I need to live vicariously through you."

"You know there's a solution to that."

But she was already shaking her head. "I can't do one-night stands. I want to, but I'm just not comfortable doing it. I can't trust people like that."

I narrowed my eyes on her then went to grab the drawing paper. Today, the kids would be drawing, then painting. "You know I don't trust people in general, given my history. Though I did take Urban to my apartment."

Her eyes widened. "*You* took *him* to your apartment? You never take anyone to your apartment."

"I know." But I didn't want to talk about what the reason for that might have been. To say there was a connection with Urban would've been an understatement, but how could I have trusted him then when I didn't even know him?

"Anyway…" I said as I pulled my phone out of my pocket. "It's almost time for the kids to arrive, so I'm going to head over to the equipment shed to get everything out. Robin's probably already wondering where I am since she doesn't have a key."

"OK," she said. I thought that'd be the end of it, then she called out, "You can paint me a picture later."

I shook my head but laughed. With my back to her, she wouldn't be able to see me smiling, but Jade and I were two peas in a pod.

Robin was leaning against the equipment shed scrolling through her phone. So far, she was the first teen counselor I'd had who hadn't complained once and genuinely seemed to like working with the kids.

"Hey, Robin. Sorry I took so long." I already had the keys in my hand and unlocked the padlock on the door. "I don't know why they won't let you have a key."

"I'm sixteen." She pushed off the side and came around to me. "I'm obviously going to steal everything inside, even though I don't play baseball or any sports, for that matter."

I snorted. She probably wasn't far off of the reason, though it didn't make sense to me. To work here, she'd had to do a background check, which meant she hadn't gotten into any trouble with the law or with her school since for the teens, the camp checked school records as well.

"I already got the cooler," she told me. It was a big, blue square that at least had wheels on it. I couldn't imagine the two of us lugging that thing down to the field along with all of the equipment. "Who's that?" she asked, making me turn to see a large man headed our way.

For a split second, I hoped it was Urban, but I pushed those thoughts away, telling myself that I didn't care if it's him or not.

Then the man got close enough for us to really see him and my heart sank.

Fucking Bryson Madden.

"He's one of the players."

"Right." She kept watching him. "But he's not one of the volunteers this year."

"No. He isn't." I shut the door to the shed but didn't fasten the lock before turning toward Bryson. "You can go grab a drink real quick if you want to." Robin took a beat then nodded. It must've been obvious that I wanted her gone for this conversation.

"Hey, Everly," he said with a toothy grin that I'd once thought was attractive. Now… not at all. It was funny how personality could completely change a person's attractiveness.

"What are you doing here?"

"I came to volunteer."

I began shaking my head before he finished tell me his reason. "You're not volunteering here this year. So no. You can't be here."

"You can always use an extra set of hands, right? If you remember correctly, I'm very good with my hands."

"You're mediocre with them at best." But I bit my lips together, wishing I could take all those words back. It wasn't smart to antagonize a guy like this. "Look, I need you to leave. This is my job and you've taken this too far."

He furrowed his brows. "You know this *playing hard to get* isn't cute."

"Great." I threw my hands in the air and let them fall until they slapped the sides of my legs. "I don't want to be cute to you and as I've told you several times, I'm not playing hard to get. I need you to leave me alone."

His jaw tightened. "Something you don't know about me," he began, "is that I don't like losing. If I want something, I'm going to get it in the end."

My heart raced and my muscles hardened, fight or flight kicking in because that sure sounded like a threat to me. It absolutely was another version of

"If I can't have you, no one can" and that never ended well.

"Leave, Bryson. And stay away from me. I will get the camp involved if I see you back here again."

Then I made a bold move and walked away.

Now I was on edge. Was I going to have to look over my shoulder for this guy forever? Surely, he'd lose interest at some point.

Luckily, I didn't have too long to think about it because Urban, his brothers, and Jenner showed up and we headed out to the field and thankfully, by then, Bryson was nowhere to be seen.

Urban slid in next to me. "Hey." He nudged my arm with his.

I didn't look over at him and forced out a "Hi."

From the corner of my eye, I could see that his eyebrows furrowed in confusion. Yeah, I'd have been confused too.

"What's wrong?" he asked, as if he suddenly knew me well enough to tell when something was wrong.

"Nothing." But my feet stopped moving.

Next to the field, there was the framing of a building with several men still working away on it. That hadn't been there yesterday when we brought them down to practice. When the baseball volunteers weren't here, the kids kind of took it upon themselves to play around. I'd learned enough doing this—still almost nothing—to help them keep score if they decided to scrimmage. And it was a great group of kids so we didn't have any problems.

"What's this?" I looked up at Urban for the first time.

Still confused, he said, "You told me you wanted an equipment shed closer to the field."

"Yeah. I did." I looked back at the men working. It was laid out behind one of the benches the kids sat on when they weren't playing. Not too close to the field, but not so far that we'd have to drag the heavy equipment anywhere. "So you… what? Just snapped your fingers and made it happen?"

"Uh…" one of the guys behind us said under his breath, which for some reason, pissed me off.

Though my tone probably should've been better. This was something nice Urban was doing for the kids. Yes. For the kids since I refused to believe that he'd done it because I'd been the one who'd said we needed it.

"Yeah." He folded his arms over his chest. Forget about the fact that he had the heavy-as-fuck equipment bag over his shoulder. He acted like it weighed nothing. "I kind of did. I didn't snap my fingers, though. I just told my mom that the camp needed it."

I sighed and pinched the bridge of my nose then did my best to at least look thankful. "Thank you. That was nice of you."

Then we started walking again. The kids got all of their energy going, grabbed their gloves, and waited for Brooks to split them up into groups again.

However this time, it was only three groups, which didn't make sense to me since there were four baseball players. Urban was talking to his brother and they were gesturing with their arms, but I couldn't hear what they were saying.

"Are you all right?" Robin asked, but when I looked at her, she looked like she was approaching a rabid animal and had to be careful.

I took a deep breath and put Bryson Madden out of my head. "Yes. I'm sorry. I'm good. I promise I won't snap at anyone again."

"Was it that baseball player?" she asked. "The one who was here first? He's not a volunteer. Did something happen?"

"Which baseball player?" Urban asked from behind me.

I slowly closed my eyes and took a deep breath.

Robin glanced at Urban, then at me, and said, "I'll take the cooler over there."

Brooks, Silas, and Jenner had the kids in their groups and paired them so that the kids were already tossing a ball back and forth to warm up.

"Which baseball player, Everly?" he asked again, but this time with a lot less patience.

There was no use trying to avoid telling him. He was going to find out because I might not have known Urban so well yet, but I did know enough to be sure that he'd storm out of here and confront Bryson if I didn't tell him anyway. This way, maybe I could lessen any blow up that would've happened otherwise.

"Bryson was here before you guys showed up this morning," I told him, then I went on to relay everything that had happened between the two of us. Not because I had to. Once again, Urban wasn't my boyfriend and didn't have the right to the details of my life. But he was a nice guy—at least to me—and he was kind of already involved in this part.

His face was made of stone, hard and solid. Honestly, I worried he'd break his own jaw. "That fucker."

"Hey." I reached out and put my hand on his arm because the man looked like he was about to come undone. "I can't have you talking like that here. There are kids around and parents aren't going to like it if their kids come home from camp swearing like sailors."

He nodded in agreement, his features softening but only slightly. "But that sure sounded like a threat." All he'd done was lower his voice. The venom was still very present.

"That's what I thought, but if he shows up again, I'll let the director know and he can take care of it. I can't have this be a problem."

"It's about to be Madden's problem."

I narrowed my eyes at him. "This isn't for you to take care of," I told him. "This is my problem and I never should've asked you to tell him to back off. It seems to have made him more determined."

"I can't just stand here and do nothing."

"Why not?" I snapped. "We're not together. Or is it that you don't like someone else sniffing around what you think is your territory?" My voice was getting a bit louder. "I'm not your territory, Urban. It was one night. Is this another case of you wanting me because you can't have me? Is it like him?"

Urban snapped back as if I'd slapped him. "I've

got news for you, Everly. I've already had you. This isn't that."

I wanted to tell him to fuck off for that comment, but this was camp and I couldn't do that. Instead, I shook my head and walked away.

It took an immense amount of effort, but I was able to avoid Urban the rest of the time they were there. We only exchanged words when it was necessary and then they were off to get ready for their game.

By the end of the day, I just wanted to get in my car and go home, but as soon as I'd started it, the phone rang. It was my sister. The one I still talked to sometimes, so I answered.

"Hey, Telly," I said. That had been her nickname since she'd been a kid. I was the youngest, so I wasn't there when she'd gotten it and for some bizarre reason that nobody ever thought to explain to me, they also didn't tell me the meaning behind it. "What's up?"

"So, I have a favor to ask…" And that was when I wished I hadn't answered the phone. "I've got rent due and my check was shorter than it should've been. Is there any way I can borrow eight hundred from you? I'll pay it back as soon as I can."

I closed my eyes and sat back against the seat with a hard thump. Fucking Typical.

"I'm all out of favors today, Telly," I told her. "And as I've said before, I can't afford to pay your rent. I have my own."

"Evie…"

"Don't call me that," I snapped. It was the nickname only used in my family when they were trying to get something out of me but it sounded like nails against a chalk board to me..

Well, today, I didn't have anything to give. I ended the call without saying goodbye.

That night after I knew the game had ended, I sat on my bed with my phone in my hand hoping Urban would call me. I could've called him but was too embarrassed over how I'd acted earlier.

Hell, I'd felt a bit guilty when the words had come out of my mouth but not enough to watch the game on TV, even though I knew that was an option.

Then he didn't call and I was more upset about that than I should've been.

As if my day could've gotten any worse.

CHAPTER 9
URBAN

The fact that Everly had compared me to Madden pissed me off to a level that I hadn't been in a very long time.

I wanted blood, though I didn't want to go to prison. I'd have to work my anger out in a different way. I took it out on the ball that night. Being pissed at Everly apparently was good for my game. I got on base every single at bat and even got a home run, driving in three runs. And every time I imagined that Madden's face was the ball.

Was it the healthiest way to deal with it? Yeah. As far as I could tell it was.

But I didn't talk to a single person in the clubhouse outside of what was mandatory when they congratulated me on a good game. I just wanted to go home and be away from everyone and no matter how much I wanted to address things with Madden, I couldn't do it in the clubhouse when I was this fucking angry.

Unfortunately, my big brother didn't see that as a necessity.

When Brooks knocked on my door, my instinct was to ignore it. Though a small part of me hoped it was Everly, I had to remind myself that she didn't know where I lived. She hadn't been here, and I hadn't told her.

Fuck. I'd barely known her a week.

As I ignored my brother on the other side of the door, he kept knocking. It wasn't like a knock here or there. His knuckles just kept hitting the door over and over again until I wanted to rip the damn thing off the hinges.

"*What?*" I spat when I finally swung the door open.

"So you're still in a good mood, then?" He walked right in without me inviting him. I supposed I wasn't going to get rid of him quickly, after all.

"*My mood* is fine. What do you want?"

Brooks shook his head and dropped onto my couch then put his feet on the coffee table.

Fucker still had his shoes on and he'd have known that was going to annoy me.

"Get your feet off the table." I sat on the other end of the couch.

"Why do you think Mom agreed to have you, Silas, and Cobb so close together?" he asked, like some sort of philosopher. No way was this why he was here.

"My guess is Dad realized that if he wanted us all to play together, he'd have to get her to pop us out one after another."

"Then why'd she wait two years to have Camden?"

I sighed, wishing he'd just get to why he was really here. "Can you fucking imagine? Four boys in, what? Five years?"

"Not even. Cobb isn't five years younger than me."

"Even worse."

"Yeah." Then silence hung between us until I gave in. Brooks was good at waiting all of us out.

"Why are you here, Brooks? Just tell me so I can go to bed."

He turned slightly on the couch but was careful to make sure that his shoes didn't touch the cushion. Listen, I wasn't a germaphobe, but I liked things clean. That was why even in my last apartment, I'd had a cleaning lady three times a week.

"What happened at camp today?" Yeah, I thought that was what this was about.

"Nothing."

"Bullshit. We couldn't hear what was being said, but Everly looked pissed and she was definitely raising her voice." He nudged my shoulder. "What'd you do?"

I gave him a disgusted look. "Why the fuck would you think *I* had done something?"

He shrugged. "Playing the odds." When I didn't answer, he added, "Listen, it's typically us players, so what'd you do?"

At least he'd had the decency to include himself in that. He wasn't lying. Professional players might be some of the best in their area, but sometimes, we were shit with relationships. It was hard. A player could be traded at any moment, like I'd been, and that wasn't easy for the family. It was one of the reasons I didn't plan on having a family until I was done playing, if I decided to have one at all.

It wasn't fair to a wife and kids for her husband to be more focused on baseball than them most of the year.

Some made it work. Others didn't.

Now the question became: Did I want to talk to Brooks about this?

The answer was *not really*, but he was the only one I *would* talk to about it. He was our secret keeper. Even from the other brothers, though the four of us had kept each other's secrets since we'd been kids.

So I took a deep breath and dove in.

"Madden was at camp today before we were," I began.

"Why? He's not one of the volunteers this year."

"Exactly." I pushed to my feet. "Do you want something to drink?" Because I needed one.

"I'll take some water."

After getting us both a bottle of water, I sat back down on my side of the couch.

"Are these reusable bottles?" Brooks asked as he unscrewed the cap.

I nodded. "Sure are. The cleaning lady makes sure they're always filled because I need something I can grab and take with me. Got to think about the environment and shit."

Brooks took a long drink then twirled his fingers so I'd keep talking.

"Anyway, he showed up and made what I think was a thinly veiled threat to Everly."

His brows slammed down. "Why would he do that? What was the threat?"

Fuck, I didn't want to talk about this. "Everly spent a night with him last year. Now he just won't leave her alone. Told her he doesn't like losing."

Brooks's jaw tightened. "And he said she's what he's losing?"

"Not specifically but he did say he'd be back because he doesn't like losing."

"Fucking threatening a woman who wants nothing to do with you. What a fucking asshole."

"Yeah, well..." I took another quick drink. "Everly got pissed at me because I said I was going to take care of it. Can't stand by and watch a woman get harassed. I'd do it for anyone."

"Right..." The sound of his voice was off, though, as if he either thought I was lying to myself that Everly was just another woman or that I wouldn't do it for anyone. I would. I'd shown that by approaching Everly in the first place.

"Anyway, she got pissed because she said it was her problem to deal with and she shouldn't have had me talk to him in the first place."

"She got that upset at you wanting to help her out?"

I groaned. That wasn't the reason and I really didn't want to say it out loud yet knew that I had to. "Not exactly. She snapped asking if I was another case of wanting something that I couldn't have which I think was comparing me to Madden." Then I let the silence hang out there until Brooks nudged me.

"And?"

"And I may have said that wasn't the case because I'd already had her."

He chuckled, which wasn't the reaction I'd thought I'd get. "You're a god-damned idiot."

"Yeah. I know. She just walked away. Haven't talked to her since."

Brooks pushed to the edge of the couch and put his elbows on his knees, as if he were trying to think up some plan to take over the world. Maybe he was trying to come up new ways to tell me I was an idiot.

"You want to talk to her, though?" He looked at me the way only a big brother could. Like he knew me so well, he could see the answer before I formed it.

"Yeah." That was at least an easy answer. "I like

her. She's funny and doesn't give fuck all about me being a player or baseball. Hell, she knows almost nothing about the game."

The corner of his mouth turned up. "You could teach her."

I shook my head. "Nah. I don't want to get attached to anyone here because I'm hopefully going to get offered a contract elsewhere."

Now he let out a loud laugh that I thought would rattle the shit off the walls, as if I'd just said the funniest thing he'd ever heard.

"Why are you laughing?" I asked once he didn't calm down.

He took a couple of breaths to get himself under control. "Two reasons. You think that now that you're here, they're going to let you leave and you think you're not already attached to this woman."

"Oh, I'm leaving." That was my end goal. I couldn't live out my career here in Kalamazoo.

He waved his hand as if he were trying to wipe the idea from my head. "There's no way, Urban. You're here now. Mom's not going to let you leave."

"She doesn't get to control that if another team has an offer."

"She's going to offer you a fuck-ton of money."

"I'll play elsewhere for less."

"Then you really are a fucking idiot," he said. I scowled. "Look, we all know that we have a limited number of years to play this game. We have to earn what we can to support our families for the rest of our lives. Sure, we'll go on and do other things, but come on. I'd be willing to bet that you already got a bump just by coming here."

That, I wasn't going to confirm. Mom *had* paid me more because it was required in my contract. She probably would've done it anyway because she's my mom.

"So, leaving would be dumb," he continued. "You can ask for anything at the end of this year and you're going to get it. The only thing Mom has to deal with is the league salary cap. She'll give you what you want. Plus, Cobb's going to be here soon. Do you really want to leave your brothers?"

I shook my head. "I don't know why everyone thinks Cobb is coming here to play. He's not. Have you talked to him? He'll quit the sport before he comes to Kalamazoo."

"Pft. No, he won't. He's just like us. He'll keep playing."

I sighed because it was hard to argue with him about that.

"And if you weren't attached to Everly already, you wouldn't care that she's pissed at you. You'd care about what Madden is doing, but you'd scare him off without talking to her about it."

Well…fuck. He wasn't wrong there.

If I let myself think about it, I was already kind of attached to Everly. Love? Nah. Definitely not. We'd only met days ago. But I'd already grown accustomed to talking to her and it didn't sit well with me that she was now angry.

Admitting all that to myself was enough for a single night.

Tomorrow we had a day game, so Brooks didn't stay too long, but I had to admit it was nice hanging out with my brother.

In Florida, I'd had friends I was with often, but it wasn't the same as being with your brothers. The guys who knew you better than anyone and had seen you at your worst and your best.

Now I had to think about whether I'd still leave the team if Cobb ended up here, which I thought was impossible.

The next day, I was at the field early like everyone else. We had a full schedule for day games. It just started a lot fucking earlier.

We played the game like we always did.

Intending to win and in the end, we did. The kids from camp were on a field trip here and I hoped they enjoyed it. I only knew because it was on the schedule my sister gave me and I looked at it in the locker room. It didn't say where they were sitting but it wasn't anywhere I could see them.

I'd looked for Everly but never found her and my focus needed to be on the game, anyway.

After we were done, before we were going to head for showers, Everly stepped out onto the field from the back wall with a group of excited ten-year-olds behind her. She looked… beautiful. She was wearing a tank top and jean shorts, much like I'd seen her at the first game she'd come to with my sister. Her legs were tan and she was wearing Converses, though it didn't look like she had socks on. Her caramel-blonde hair was pulled up into a wavy ponytail and she was wearing sunglasses, so I couldn't see her eyes.

I really needed to stop taking inventory like a fucking creeper.

The kids from camp were meeting the entire team. Or at least those of us who'd played today. They were also getting a chance to throw the ball around in the outfield and run the bases.

It wasn't something we did often, I was told, but

for Grandpa's camp, the team would make all kinds of exceptions.

The kids were at least patient with us and once the crowd around me had dissipated a little and the kids were lining up to play catch with some of the players, I slid in next to Everly but kept my eyes out on the activity so it'd just look like we were standing there together casually.

"Hey," I said, trying to keep up the casual appearance.

"Hi." At least this time, she didn't sound so angry. "You didn't call me last night." Then, as if she realized what she'd said, she added, "Not that you have to. It's just that I kind of got used to it this week."

"I didn't think you'd want me to."

A small sigh came from beside me. "That's my fault. I'm sorry I snapped at you at camp. Yesterday was… a lot."

"Want to tell me about it?"

Then she stepped in front of me and pushed her sunglasses up onto the top of her head. Everly wasn't very tall and I was pretty sure that if I pulled her into my arms right then, I'd be able to rest my head on top of hers.

"Not here," she told me, but that didn't mean

she didn't want to tell me. I quickly glanced around to see if Madden was out here. He wasn't. He hadn't played today, so he'd been able to hit the clubhouse as soon as we'd been done. Though if he weren't such a fucker, he would've stayed to meet the kids anyway.

"Somewhere else?"

Everly bit into her bottom lip for a split second before saying, "You're done after this, right?" I nodded. "Why don't you come to my apartment and I'll cook for you? We can talk about it there if you want to. You're not obligated to."

I chuckled and shook my head. "I know I'm not obligated to, but I did ask."

"Yeah." Something flashed across her face that I didn't recognize. "You did."

"Then I'll see you there."

Now I had incentive to hurry up because I'd get to her house in record time. Though thinking about her and the last time I'd been in her apartment while in the shower in the clubhouse was a bad idea, so I did my best to keep all thoughts away from Everly.

At least for now.

It'd only been a few days since I'd had sex with her, but I was more than ready to do it again. That wasn't why I was going to her apartment, but if that was where it led, I wouldn't complain.

First, I wanted to talk to her. Hear why her day yesterday had been so fucked.

And if we didn't end up naked, that'd be fine.

I'd be happy if I only got to hold her for a little while.

And that was how I knew I was royally screwed.

CHAPTER 10
EVERLY

I knew I was walking into danger by inviting Urban to my apartment again.

I just didn't seem to care.

There was an undeniable pull toward him, a feeling of safety that I hadn't had in a while—if ever, which was ridiculous, given that I hadn't known him long.

Yet I couldn't deny it was happening.

It was like I wanted to see how close I could walk to the fire without getting burned because, in the end, we all knew I would be the one getting burned. It was always me.

After we were done on the field, we took a bus back to the camp where parents were already waiting for us, so all the kids were gone as soon as we got off the bus. Which meant I could go home and get cleaned up. It wasn't an overly hot day, so I wasn't all sweaty and I wouldn't have to shower.

As soon as I got home, I kicked my shoes off and hurried to the kitchen. I'd already planned my dinner—it would now just be for two, which was what I'd been planning to do anyway. I always made more than I'd eat so I'd have leftovers for the next day.

First, I turned the oven on to preheat then washed my hands really well. Once that was started, I pulled the chicken breasts out of the fridge, covering them with seasoning before setting them on the small cooking sheet. Next were the potatoes. They needed to be sliced, but not all the way through. These were going in the air fryer. I could do the salad and green beans after I cleaned up.

Now that everything was started, I ran through my apartment to the bathroom, where I used a washcloth to clean up. My armpits needed freshening and I wanted as much of the sunscreen off as I could manage without an actual shower. When that wasn't going well, I hopped in the damn shower.

It was the quickest of my life and I made sure not to get my hair wet.

Then I hurried to my room for clothes. I chose another tank top and jean shorts that were very similar to what I'd worn earlier. I also needed a quick stop back in the bathroom to take my hair down and make it look like it hadn't been in a ponytail all day.

I was just finishing up when there was a knock on my door. My stomach somersaulted over itself. I'd seen this guy naked. I shouldn't have been nervous for him to be here.

It wasn't nerves at all and I knew it. I just wasn't going to admit it to myself.

"Hi," I said as I opened the door.

"Hi." Urban came in carrying a round container and toed his shoes off at the door.

"What is that?" I asked him while pointing at the container he carried.

"Dessert. I wanted to bring something."

I pushed to my toes to get a look, which made him lower his hand.

"Is that an ice cream cake?"

"Yeah."

I furrowed my brows and shut the door behind us. "I love ice cream cake. How did you know that I love ice cream cake?"

The corners of his mouth turn up, but it didn't

turn into a full smile. "I asked my sister if she could find out. She asked your friend, then I bought an ice cream cake."

It wasn't a large one, thank god, because I would eat the whole thing after he left tonight. This way, there was a decent chance that he'd help me eat it.

"Let's put it in the freezer until we're ready for it."

Urban followed me into the kitchen and put the cake in the freezer. "It smells so good in here."

"Thank you. If there's one thing I can do, it's cook."

He raised an eyebrow. "There's definitely more than one thing."

I snorted. "I'm making roasted chicken, garlic herb potatoes, roasted green beans, and a salad. Is there anything else you'd like?"

"That sounds like plenty."

Before I responded, I yanked the fridge open so that I could pull out the things that I needed. "I like to have two vegetables for dinner," I told him. "I figure it balances the ice cream cake I'm going to eat later."

He chuckled. "I eat a ton of vegetables, so it's good for me. What do you want me to do?"

"Nothing," I said right away. "I invited you here."

"Yeah, but I can be helpful." He went over the sink and began washing his hands. "I'll be honest. I don't do much in the kitchen usually, but I'll do whatever you want me to."

"Yeah." I nodded. "OK. You could start making the salad." I pointed a toe toward the fridge. "Everything is on the bottom shelf."

"Great."

While I worked on the green beans, he brought everything to the counter at the cutting board.

"Do you like to cook?" he asked as he worked.

"Yeah. I like eating more, but I figured if I wanted to eat well, I had to learn how to cook well."

He chuckled. "I had someone cook for me in Florida."

I raised an eyebrow as I poured some extra virgin olive oil on the beans. "Like a personal chef?"

"Yeah. Basically. Though she'd make things ahead so that I could heat it up when I got home."

"So you had to fire the person?"

He nodded. "It was through a service so I used the app to cancel."

I snickered. "I guess there really is an app for everything. What do you do now that you're here?"

"So far, order out. But I'm looking for someone." He eyed me tossing the green beans in the oil then grabbing the salt and pepper to season. "Are you looking for a new job?"

I chuckled because there was a time that I'd toyed with the idea of being a chef, but I just didn't have it in me. "You might not like my cooking," I told him. "Everyone has their own taste."

"I like how you taste," he said. I was about to chastise him when he added, "I meant I'm going to like how yours tastes." Then he winced. "That doesn't actually sound better."

At least while we cooked, we laughed, and then finally, once everything was done, I plated it the way I wanted it to look then took it to the table. Urban had already taken the salad and dressing out there, as well as our utensils and drinks.

It felt so good to sit down that I sighed.

"Tired?" he asked.

"Not really. It just feels good to relax."

"Yeah. It does." He took his first bite of the chicken and I waited. He shut his eyes and made a satisfied sound. "Damn."

"Good?"

"Seriously, are you looking for a new job?" he asked. "I pay very well."

I snickered. "Actually, I'm not. I love my job." Then I shrugged. "Or jobs, rather."

We each took another bite when he asked, "So you said you wanted to talk more privately. This is the most private we can get."

I let out a sigh. That was right. I had said I wanted to talk about it somewhere else. "You didn't call last night and I don't know. I guess I'd kind of expected it. Though I probably shouldn't have." Though that had been just the cherry on the crap sundae.

His shoulders tightened, which wasn't what I'd meant to happen. I wasn't trying to make him feel bad, but that had been kind of a letdown last night.

"You were pissed at me earlier."

"I was," I agreed. "That was my fault and I'm sorry. I shouldn't have taken my frustration out on you. I didn't mean what I said."

Urban reached out and stroked a thumb over my cheek as his other fingers curled under my chin. "Yeah, well, I could've worded things better."

Yeah. He could have.

"That's not what started it, though." I took a drink and then a deep breath. "First Bryson showed up—again. Which I told you about at camp. Then I was pissy with you"—I gave him an apologetic look —"and that sucked because you're always nice to me and I shouldn't lash out."

"Forget about it," he told me as he stuffed a couple of green beans into his mouth. "It happens."

"But then I was in a worse mood and when I was leaving for the day. My sister Telly called and wanted money."

He stopped eating and looked me in the eye. "Why is your sister asking you for money?"

Right. That was going to lead into a whole family discussion. "That's how my family is. Or most of my family. I have one sister I don't talk to at all, another I talk to sometimes and she asks me for money a lot. My brother and I are sort of close and he doesn't ask me for things. Then there are my parents, who think that I'm supposed to hand over whatever anyone needs because I make more money than they do."

He furrowed his brows. "Did you give it to her?"

"No," I said with a touch of outrage that he thought I'd do that. "I didn't give it to her. Despite what people think, teachers aren't highly paid."

"No one thinks that."

I snorted. "My family thinks that."

"Then they're idiots."

Well, that, I couldn't disagree with. "Anyway. It was one crappy thing after another, and I'm glad that day is over."

"Sounds like you need ice cream cake," he told me, as if I hadn't just dumped my family drama on him. The fact that he didn't ask any follow-up questions made me warm inside. I didn't want to tell him why I didn't talk to my sister anymore. I didn't want to be put in a position to defend any of them because I wouldn't, yet I also didn't want someone else shitting all over them.

My relationship with my family was complicated at best, toxic at worst. It was the reason I didn't see them much.

"Let me clean this up and we can bring it out."

When I stood to clear the table, Urban did too. He helped me clear, scrape, and load the dishwasher. I wouldn't turn it on until later tonight because it wasn't full yet. Then we went back to the table with the ice cream cake.

I was going to grab plates but figured that it was small enough that we could share it as it was. Two forks were all we needed and our drinks were still on the table.

Urban sat back in his chair and I pulled mine over to the corner next to him so that we could both reach the cake. Then I folded one leg under me.

"You first," he said, indicating the cake.

I took a normal-sized spoonful. The ice cream melted into a creamy goodness in my mouth.

"This is what I needed," I told him. "I'm not even hungry anymore. This is for the soul."

He chuckled. "Well, I'm glad I could satisfy your soul."

I took two more bites before broaching the subject that I knew we needed to talk about. "I don't want you asking your sister to find out things about me."

He stopped and cocked his head to the side, a spoonful of ice cream cake in front of him. "Why not?"

I wet my suddenly dry lips. "I don't want anyone to think we're dating. We probably shouldn't be seen together in public, either. Today was fine because it was a camp outing, but in general."

"We *are* dating. It's casual but we're dating."

I sat up straight. "No we're not. I don't date."

"What do you call this, Everly?" he asked. "Do you make dinner for all your one-nighters?"

"Well, no—"

"Did you talk to any of them every night?"

I sighed because I hated where this was going. He wasn't wrong, which meant it'd have to end. "No."

"So we're dating." He shrugged. "It's not a big deal. It doesn't change anything. I'm not looking for anything serious so you don't have to freak out."

I went back to the ice cream cake so that I'd have something to do and I didn't want it to melt. "But I can't date, Urban. It's not something I'm willing to do."

He furrowed his brows again. "But you are." Then he sat back. "Do you at least want to tell me why you don't think you date?"

Though I wanted to argue the wording of his question, I wasn't going to. It wouldn't matter in the end because he was right. This sure did feel like a date when you put a romantic spin on it.

"Not really," I said honestly. "It's kind of embarrassing."

He shook his head. "Probably not for you."

He was wrong on that, but I'd tell him anyway. "My first serious boyfriend my freshman year in college… He was…" I swallowed hard. "Like my first, first." There was no reason to hide it. "We'd been together for a month, and I brought him home at Christmas for my sanity and I warned him about my family."

"They didn't like him?"

"It wasn't that. Actually, one of them liked him *too* much." My gaze went to the cake so I wouldn't have to look at him when I said this. "My sister Janelle—she's the one I don't talk to… I walked in on the two of them fucking in the basement."

"Shit."

"Yeah. Shit. I still had to ride back to school with him. The entire time he said he was sorry. He couldn't help himself. She was just…" Again, I had to swallow. "Better than me. Not in general, but apparently at sex."

"That's bullshit."

I shrugged. "I didn't know what I was doing. He was the first person I'd been with, but yeah… It was embarrassing for me. Not for him."

His spoon made a sound on the table, then his hand slid along my jaw and forced my head up so that I'd have to look at him.

"That's embarrassing for *him*. If you didn't know what you were doing and wanted to learn, he should've taught you. Not fucked your sister."

I nodded. There'd been more to it than that, at least to me there had been, but I didn't want to get into it. Urban removed his hand, but it looked like he'd done so reluctantly.

"I waited two years before I had a serious boyfriend again. It was going into my senior year. I had an apartment. Things were going to be great. I'd started dating him in the summer. Things were good, I thought."

"Then?" Because he clearly knew the other shoe was going to drop.

"Then I found out that he had put everything in my apartment on the marketplace and was trying to organize people picking things up all on the same day, so when I got home, everything would just be gone."

"*What?*" he said, a little too loudly.

"Yeah. I found out because a friend saw the listings. He was arrested, but I didn't follow up to see what came of it."

"Well, fuck, Everly. That alone would definitely have you swear off men."

"Yeah, well, strike three came in the form of my last semi-serious boyfriend. I was cautious. Thought I'd done my due diligence. Then I discovered he'd started sleeping with one of the teachers at my school. This was two years ago."

"The school you teach at now?" he asked. I nodded. "Does she still work there?"

I snorted. "Yup. She works there. They're married, so I still see him from time to time. I don't really care because if he cheated on me, he'll cheat on her, but like it's hard working with someone you can't trust."

"I bet it is. So those are the three strikes," he said softly. I nodded. "And you've sworn off men?"

"No. Clearly, I haven't sworn off men. You're here, aren't you?"

"I am."

"I've sworn off relationships. The minute my heart gets involved, I know it's going to get broken."

The silence hung between us until he said, "Well, fuck."

"I mean… it sucked," I told him. "I'm over it. Not pining for any of those losers, but it's made me guard my heart."

"Clearly." He sat forward and set his hand on my thigh. "But even if I'm not looking to make you fall in love with me, it makes everything a fuck of a lot harder for the rest of us."

**CHAPTER 11
URBAN**

*E*verly's lips parted, as if she were surprised by what I'd said. *Fuck. I* was surprised by what I'd said. Yet it was something that had to be said.

The shit men she'd been with before had made it a fuck of a lot harder for anyone else who might want a chance with Everly. A relationship hadn't been something that I'd wanted when I'd met her and I wasn't sure it was something that I wanted now.

What I didn't want was for it to be off limits for at least the time that I was here.

There was something about Everly that sucked me in. It wasn't just the sex, even if that had been spectacular. It was the fact that she didn't seem to want anything from me and that was really fucking different.

The major downside was that I didn't plan on staying in Kalamazoo and couldn't ask her if she'd be willing to leave with me.

After knowing her a week, it'd be real fucking creepy to ask that question when we didn't know where this would go. Well, she thought she knew, given the number of times she'd mentioned us being friends after we slept together.

Were we friends? I'd say *yes*, given that I'd called her every night and the one that I hadn't, I'd wanted to so fucking badly.

"What's that supposed to mean?" she finally asked.

"It means…" I reached out and yanked her chair so that it landed between my legs, bringing her so much closer. "That those other fuckers screwing you over made it hard for anyone else who might want you. They made sure that any other man would have to work twice as hard. But you know what?"

"What?" she whispered.

"I don't necessarily think that's a bad thing."

Her eyes widened. "You don't?"

I shook my head. "Any man who's going to be

with you should want to work hard to prove that he isn't like them. That he's not going to hurt you."

"Or fuck my sister?" she whispered, but there was something playful behind it.

"Or fuck your sister," I agreed. That wasn't something I could imagine doing to anyone I'd been with even if it'd been casual. That shit caused too much drama.

Without waiting for her to say anything else, I wrapped my hand around the back of her neck and pulled her to me so that I could kiss her.

Even Everly's kisses felt different. Her mouth was warm and wet. Her kisses full of confidence, even when the softest lips I could imagine. Given everything she'd just told me, a lack of confidence wouldn't have been a surprise, but she didn't have that.

Or at least she didn't show it.

When I took the kiss deeper, Everly climbed into my lap and straddled me. I pushed her into my erection so she'd feel exactly how she affected me. I wanted her to know. More than that, I wanted her to know that I wouldn't screw her over, but I'd leave that until after.

Without pulling my mouth from hers, I pushed the chair back and stood, taking her with me. I was able to walk us to her bedroom without a problem. For once in my life, I could almost be thankful to my dad for forcing us to stay in shape. Everly wasn't big, though she also wasn't too thin, but I liked being able to carry her to the bedroom.

Once there, I was able to set her on the bed on her knees and that was when I pulled back to yank her shirt over her head.

It was like that was the catalyst that ignited the fire because it was a storm of us removing each other's clothes and I had no idea where any of it went. I also didn't care.

Everly kept her gaze on mine until she couldn't as she lay down on her stomach and took my cock in her mouth. Fucking hell.

She slid her wet mouth down and then back, using her hand with it. Her head bobbed back and forth until I was about to cum in her mouth. That was when I had to stop it. That wasn't how I wanted this to end.

It was easy to flip her around and push her legs open so that I could bury my face there. The groan she released when I licked her the first time was more than worth it.

I could do this forever if it meant hearing her.

The sounds she made were mostly small gasps

as her fingers dug into my scalp. The sting was good and pushed me to do more.

"Urban," she said in a breath, which I knew meant she was close. Her clit hardened under my tongue as a sign for me to keep doing exactly what I was doing and within another few seconds, her muscles tightened, her legs pressed against the sides of my head and the rush of excitement flowing through her.

It wasn't until she relaxed back and pushed at my head that I even thought about stopping.

I quickly wiped a hand over my mouth before I kissed her.

That had even almost been too much for me. I'd almost released right onto her blanket. If it would've lasted any longer, I probably would have.

But I wanted inside of Everly.

After I grabbed one of her condoms—because I remembered that she preferred to use her own—I slid that down me on the walk back to the bed.

"Up on the bed," I told her. She'd been at the edge and I wanted her in the middle. After doing exactly what I'd commanded, I climbed over her and watched myself disappear into her.

Everly let out a sigh as her head dropped back. I

took that as a sign that it felt as good for her as it did for me.

The first time, I'd been looking at her back, but this time, I wanted to see her face. The pleasure she was feeling pushed me toward my release, but I was going to hold out as long as possible.

Her hands trailed up my back and I had to close my eyes to keep from cumming. Every touch of hers was threatening to send me.

I coaxed one more orgasm out of her before I allowed myself to go.

And once I had, I didn't want to move a muscle. Yet I couldn't crush her, either. Instead, I rolled over onto the other side of the bed to catch my breath.

"I'll say one thing about us," she said breathlessly. "We're good at that."

"Hell, yes, we are." I left out the fact that it hadn't felt like that with anyone else in my life.

"You can use the bathroom first," she said, though I wanted to stay right where we were for a while. Cuddling after didn't seem to be Everly's thing. It wasn't really my thing usually, but in this case, I wanted to stay with her.

I guessed that cuddling not being something I was into had more to do with who I was with.

When I came out of the bathroom, Everly had

her robe on again and was standing by the dresser. It was a clear message that she was ready for me to leave. I collected my clothes and put them on, but I didn't rush. She stood over there with her hands folded under her breasts, which were covered by a red silk robe, looking a little impatient.

That thing did nothing but turn me on some more.

Another time, maybe.

"Thanks for tonight," she said quietly and it sounded like she meant more than the great sex we'd just had.

"You're welcome, but next time, we're doing this at my place so *I* can kick *you* out." I'd meant it as a joke and hoped she'd take it that way but I'd also wanted to point out that she was constantly making me leave her.

She snorted. "I'll be gone before you have the chance to kick me out."

That comment burned in my stomach. It certainly didn't sit well. She was so injured from her past that she really couldn't see a future in anything.

I'd make it my mission to change her mind. Not all of us were bad and sure, I might not have wanted a forever thing with her since I was leaving, I did want her to be happy in the end. Maybe I could get her to be open to something more with a man in the future.

Everly walked me to the door and while she made no move to kiss me goodbye, I gently pinched her chin between my thumb and finger, then lifted it to press my lips to hers quickly.

Then the door shut behind me.

The next day was another day game, which meant early to the field. The team was looking good and I wasn't all that worried about today's game. Though I was so tempted to call my sister and get her to bring Everly to the game, I didn't do it. I remembered that Everly said she didn't want me going through my sister for anything more about her.

That was hard for me. I had a resource to find out the information I wanted, but it was more important that I respect Everly's boundary, given the fact that so many hadn't respected any boundary.

Instead, for the first time in my life, I ordered her some flowers to be delivered immediately. This way, she'd know I was thinking about her. I knew her apartment number and looked on line for the rest of the address. Then I stepped out into the hall to call her but decided on Facetime because I wanted to see her.

"Hey," she answered, sounding out of breath and her face was slightly flushed.

"Did you just go for a run?" I asked.

She laughed, as if what I'd just asked was the most ridiculous thing in the world. "I don't go for runs, Urban. I do yoga and Pilates. I go for walks. Running and I don't get along."

"Yoga and Pilates?" I repeated and she nodded. "That explains a lot."

She giggled again. "I'm not going to ask what you mean by that."

I wet my bottom lip. "Probably better that you don't."

She let out a breath. "Don't you have a game today? Should you be getting ready for that?"

"I do have a game." What the fuck was this feeling in my stomach? I didn't get nervous to ask a woman out or to do anything. This was fucking new. "I thought I'd see if you want to come."

She furrowed her brows. "To the game?" I nodded. Happiness or whatever had been on her face slowly fell. "Remember what I said about being seen in public?"

Yeah. I did and I didn't love it. "It's not like you'd be on the field with me."

"I didn't mean—"

"I just thought you might want to come, Everly. If you don't, that's fine. Camden is coming and you could sit with her unless you don't want to be seen in public with my sister either. She's using our Dad's season tickets and said she was coming alone, so she has plenty room."

"I'll come," she said quickly, then she glanced at something behind her. "I have plenty of time. If Camden doesn't mind, I'll meet her there." She was about to say something else, but then said, "I can message her myself. Sorry. You don't have to do that."

"I don't mind talking to my sister."

"I didn't meant that," she said quickly. "I just meant… Never mind. I don't know what I meant. I'll talk to Camden and meet her there."

"Thank you." Because I did really want her there today when I probably shouldn't have. Tomorrow we had off, but only because it was a travel day. Luckily, it was just a three-game stand in Texas, and then we'd be back, but I wanted to see her before we left.

When I got back into the clubhouse, my

brothers were sitting on either side of my chair. I shook my head because they were obviously up to something. Now, I just had to wait for them to tell me what that was.

"So…" Silas began. "Still looking to leave at the end of the season?"

I glanced around because that wasn't information I necessarily wanted the entire team to know. Others could think that I wasn't dedicated to this team because of my desire to leave it when that wasn't the case.

I'd give everything I had to the Knights until I was no longer here.

Luckily, most of the rest of the guys were gone or busy with their own shit, so they weren't paying attention. Even Madden was engrossed in his phone.

Just looking at that guy pissed me off.

"Why wouldn't I?" I yanked my shirt over my head to change for the game.

"Seems like there might be something to keep you here now," Brooks added.

I snorted. "Nothing's keeping me here."

"Not even Everly?" Jenner asked, which yeah… Of course, he was up to date on everything.

"Fuck off," I muttered, but I also didn't deny it.

This wasn't the place for me to explore my feelings for Everly, whatever they were.

"Are you talking about Everly Rose?" Madden asked and all of my muscles tightened. I didn't like her name in his mouth. When I didn't answer he looked up from his phone and said, "If you are, give it up. That woman as a hard exterior that goes far beyond the hard candy coating."

"Shut up, Madden," Brooks warned. Being my brother, he'd be able to read my reaction easily.

Madden held his hands up, as if he were the innocent party here. "Hey, I'm just giving a teammate a warning. Don't waste your time on Everly Rose. Good pussy. Impenetrable exterior."

I didn't think before I acted when I lunged, ready to kill Madden with my bare hands. Chaos ensued. Guys jumped between us. Suddenly there were a lot more players in the clubhouse than before.

Unfortunately, I wasn't able to get my hands on him. Brooks and Silas jumped in front of me right before I got to him. I pushed against them, but the two of them together made it impossible.

"The fuck is wrong with you?" Madden yelled. He stepped toward me, but a couple of our other teammates got between us, though they weren't holding him back the way my brothers were holding me. "I'm helping you not waste your fucking time."

"Shut your mouth, Madden," Silas snapped.

"*You're* the fucking problem," I yelled at Madden.

It took a lot of effort, but my brothers were able to push me out of the clubhouse into the hall and they didn't let go of me until we were out there.

"What're you thinking?" Brooks asked with the harsh "Dad" tone he sometimes used with us. "You can't fight in the clubhouse."

"Yeah." Silas shook his head. "Even with Mom running the place, that's going to get you in trouble."

"I don't fucking care," I raged as I began to pace. "Let it."

"Listen." Brooks pulled me to a stop. "Hulking out on Madden isn't going to do you any good."

"You don't understand," I told him.

"I do." Silas raised his hand, like he was still in school. "If that fuck nut even *thought* about Amity, I'd want to rip his head off."

"Exactly."

"But I'd have to do it outside of the clubhouse. We need to be a team in there."

I mashed my teeth together so hard, I thought I might break a few.

But Silas was right. No matter what else happened, we had to play like a team. At this point, I could only hope that Madden started to suck so Mom would want to get rid of him. I couldn't hope for an injury because that brought bad mojo.

"I'm fine," I told them as I shook Brooks off. By the looks on their faces, they didn't believe me. "I'm fine," I said again, but this time, it sounded more like I was actually fine.

Once they were convinced, they let me back in the clubhouse.

At least Madden kept his fucking mouth shut so that I could focus on getting ready for the game.

And Everly would be there, so I couldn't suck.

CHAPTER 12
EVERLY

"I like you with my brother," Camden said from beside me as the game raged in front of us. She'd called this a pitching duel. There weren't a lot of runs and she'd explained it meant that the pitchers were determining the game. Both pitchers were good and not allowing runs, so it'd come down to whoever screwed up first.

"I'm not with your brother."

She raised her eyebrow. Camden's hair was dark, like her brothers', though she had a lot of definition in the color that probably came from highlights, but it looked so natural on her. Her hazel eyes were beautiful in the sun and probably all the other time as well. But on the sides, the little starbursts of color around her pupils really shone brightly in the natural light.

"You're not?" She cocked her head to the side. "He's never wanted anyone else at his games that I know of."

That couldn't have been true. "I'm sure he's wanted people at his games."

"Oh, you're right. Let me rephrase that. There's never been another *woman* he's wanted at his game."

"High school?"

She shook her head. "Don't get me wrong. Lots of girls showed up for him in high school. Tons. But he never asked a single one to be there."

"Past girlfriends?" There had to have been someone.

"Nope. He had girlfriends here or there in high school, but he never cared if they came or not." She rolled her eyes. "They always came and then would get pissy that his attention was on the game and not on them exaggeratingly supporting him."

I snorted as I pictured that. "Why would they think the focus would be on them?"

She looked over at me with a wide grin. "And that's why I like you with my brother. You know shit about this game, but you know it's his life. You won't put pressure on him to choose between you and it."

"I wouldn't." At least she was right about that. "But again, we're friends. I'm not with him."

She narrowed her eyes to me. "Friends who have sex, right?" My lips parted in surprise because I couldn't believe she'd just said that. Camden held up a hand to stop whatever I was going to say. "Look, the last thing I want to do is think about any of my brothers having sex." She gagged, like she was going to throw up to drive her point home. "But the fact is you're sleeping with him, right?" I bit my lips together because I wasn't going to answer that. "Friends who have sex can very quickly turn into something else. For you and Urban, I like that."

There was nothing I could say to that because I'd thought the same thing. The only difference was that I'd shut those thoughts down. There couldn't be more for Urban and me. I'd been burned too many times and refused to be again. Somehow, I knew that with Urban, the burn would be so much worse.

Instead, I asked questions about the game. If I was going to be around this in any capacity, I should at least learn a thing or two.

Kalamazoo lost that game because the reliever had walked two in a row, and then someone hit a double, driving in runs in the ninth, and the Knights hadn't responded.

That was how Camden had put it. I'd take her word for it.

Once it was over, she and I took the tunnel that I was now becoming familiar with. It would lead us down to the clubhouse, where we'd wait for Urban to come out.

A pretty woman with auburn hair who looked to be about my age was coming in the other direction. She was wearing shorts, a Kalamazoo Knights T-shirt, and sandals. It took me a full minute to realize it was Amity, Silas' girlfriend that I'd met at the game I'd gone to.

"They're going to be in a great mood," she said when she came to a stop by us. We were standing in the middle of the tunnel—or hallway.

"No kidding," Camden told her, then she turned toward me. "So." Camden clapped her hands together, like she was about to drop a conspiracy theory on us or tell us something we weren't going to want to hear. "Have either of you thought about coming to the overnight at the stadium?"

It was a new thing that Camden had organized this year. It'd be a first. On Thursday night, the kids who'd signed up for baseball camp—even if it wasn't this round—were getting the chance to spend the night at the ballpark. They were going to be camping on the field and were all very excited about it.

"Well, since I work the baseball camp," I told her, "it's kind of part of my job." Though I could've opted out of it, I didn't want to disappoint the kids.

She turned to Amity. "What about you? It'll be fun. Harlowe's coming to help chaperone. I'll be there." She motioned her hand toward me. "Everly will be there and you two will get to hang out again as you should."

Amity raised an eyebrow out of curiosity, and I wished that Camden hadn't said that.

"Please come," she added. She folded her hands in front of her so Amity would know that she was begging.

"Fine, fine. I'll come. I'm not on this away trip, anyway."

Camden bounced up and down on her toes. "Thank you, thank you, thank you."

Amity's phone dinged. As she looked at it, she said, "The guys get back on Thursday, though there's no game, so when your brother is pissed that I'm here, I'm sending him to you."

"Pft. I can handle Silas." And I believed that she could.

"I have to go." Amity started to walk away then turned back.

I waved, then Camden began leading me away.

"You know, Urban should just get you your own pass. You know how to get down there."

"If you don't want—"

Camden held up her hand to stop me. "I don't have a problem with it. It'd just be more convenient for you."

"Aren't passes for family?"

"And girlfriends."

"I'm not his girlfriend."

She quickly raised her eyebrows but it was clear she didn't believe me. "Mmm."

I wasn't. And I'd keep telling myself that.

Camden disappeared once Urban had shown up. She said she had some other brothers to harass. Now it was time for dinner. He gave me his address and said to meet him there but I took as much time as humanly possible to get there.

We ordered in to eat at his apartment. It was my

first time there and I didn't know what I was expecting, but it hadn't been this apartment.

It was large, which of course it would have been, but it was so clean. He had to have someone come in to do that, right? He opened the door wearing jeans and a dark-blue T-shirt that fit him very well. His hair was a bit messy, probably because he hadn't done much with it after he'd showered off after the game. He also wasn't wearing shoes, so when I stepped in, I kicked mine off as well.

I didn't wear outside shoes in my apartment, either.

"This place is huge," I told him as I came in. Dinner was waiting on the island in the kitchen area, which I could see, given the open concept.

"It's not mine," he said.

"What does that mean?"

"It's the team's. My mom put me here when I got traded. I'm still looking for my own place." Right, he'd only been back a short time. "It's rough. We don't have a lot of off time, as you know. I'm thinking about having Camden find me something. She knows what I like. You could help her."

I froze and didn't move any further into the apartment. But then, I forced my muscles to relax and pretended like he hadn't said what he'd just said. Helping find his apartment was too personal. Too much like what a girlfriend would do.

"If you're leaving at the end of the season, why more?" I asked as if his comment hadn't thrown me for a loop.

He shrugged. "I'd be more comfortable in my own place. I'm way too old for my mom to be choosing where I live. Plus, when I'm traded at the end of the year, I'll have some time before I have to report to spring training. I'll need somewhere to keep my shit while I look for a new place."

So either way he was leaving at the end of the season. Maybe he'd be back a little but he'd definitely be gone. That made him a safe bet. How could I get attached to someone I knew was leaving? I couldn't.

As he got our takeout from the bag, he grabbed plates. We'd ordered a bunch of Chinese and could make up our plates right there on the island.

"Your sister said today was a tough loss," I said as I watched him move around the kitchen.

"It was." He sighed. "Can't win them all, I guess." He stopped with his hands pressed against the countertop on the island. "Are you learning the game now that you've come to a few?"

I shrugged. "I guess a little. Like, I know three outs. Four balls, and you walk. Obviously, I know three strikes and you're out. But an older guy near us called *can of corn* when a player hit a ball and I have no idea what the hell that means."

He snorted then handed me a plate. "It's an old term. It comes from when women wore aprons all the time. She'd go to the store, right? Not be able to reach something."

"I'm familiar with that."

"Well, she'd use something else to knock it down—like a can of corn—and catch it easily in her apron. So if a guy pops up a ball and the player on the field doesn't even have to move to catch it, it's a can of corn."

I cocked my head to the side. "I guess that makes a little sense."

He chuckled, but then we made our plates and took them to the table. Again, I was going to ignore how normal this felt. Given that it seemed like we both wanted a friendship along with the sex, it shouldn't have been weird, but it absolutely was.

"You leave tomorrow, right?" I asked.

"Yeah. Short road trip. We've got a few in a row this month, but we come back Thursday. You busy?"

"Yeah, I have the camp overnight at the park on Thursday."

"That's right."

"I saw Amity today when Camden was bringing me down to the clubhouse. She's going to volunteer with us. Camden encouraged it."

Urban chuckled as if he knew exactly how his sister encourages things. It's not pushy but it is convincing. "Yeah? She's great. I can't believe Silas finally got her," he said. When I furrowed my brows, he added, "He's loved her since… Well, who the fuck knows when, but a long fucking time. But her brother was Silas's best friend, so…" So it was hands off. That was the unspoken rule. "Her brother died in a car accident when they were teenagers. Silas blamed himself for a long time and couldn't get out of his own way. Then Amity started working for the team and he couldn't keep himself away."

"That's kind of a sweet story. Minus her brother dying. I'm sorry to hear that." And I couldn't imagine if something happened to my brother since he was the only member of my family I was remotely close to. We weren't best friends, but we both saw the rest of them for what they were.

"Yeah. It was rough. We all played on the same

team in school. He was a good guy."

To change the subject, I said, "Amity told us that you were all going to be in great moods because of the loss. Sarcastically, of course, but you don't seem to be all that upset."

He shrugged as he took a bite of noodles. "I'll work my frustration out on you in a bit."

Tiny prickles raced across my skin. "I look forward to it."

And boy, did he…

As I'd promised him the last time we'd been at my apartment, I left before he had a chance to throw me out. Not that he would've. He'd only said that because he didn't love that when the sex was over, he could go and I'd made that clear.

Deep down, I wanted to stay. For the first time in a long time, I wanted to be wrapped up in a man's arms, our naked bodies pressed together all night.

And that was exactly why I had to leave.

With him going on a road trip tomorrow, we'd get a little space.

Something I thought we needed, yet it was something I absolutely didn't want.

Though I wouldn't admit it to myself… I was totally screwed.

CHAPTER 13
EVERLY

The days that Urban was gone were busy. First, we had to prep for the overnight at the park. Camden was so damn excited about it, given that this was her baby and it was actually happening for the first time. Along with the fact that she saw this as girls' night out as well. She was adamant that I was going to love her friend Harlowe and Amity. As if after this night together, we'd be lifelong friends.

If I was being honest with myself, I kind of needed more friends.

Jade would always be my ride or die and nothing was going to change that, but she had a life outside of me. Any other friends of mine had either moved away or we'd grown apart. It happened.

For example, this week, Jade was on vacation with her family. They did this every year. Actually, she'd be gone a couple of weeks because this was their annual trip to the Caribbean. Every year she asked me to go and I always said *no*. It didn't sit well with me, butting in on their family time, even if her parents said they considered me one of the family. She made sure the camp knew she'd be gone and they made this two weeks a break between her art sessions.

Though I had gone with them several times when we'd been younger and to say that everything had been five stars was an understatement. Another counselor named Lucia and I were the only counselors going to the overnight. It was only twenty kids and with Camden there, we were covered. Amity and Harlowe were volunteers, but actual camp people had to go, given that this was a camp event.

"Are we all set?" Lucia asked Thursday afternoon. Lucia was in her thirties, and she worked for the camp year-round. In the winter, they spent time planning for the summer, getting people to sign up, and doing a bunch of other things I wouldn't have wanted to do.

"I think so. I have all of the pop-up tents loaded

into the trailer. The kids will bring their stuff with them. I have a bag packed. Yours is in there, too."

"Well, I have both coolers packed." She placed her hand on one of the huge, blue coolers that thankfully had wheels. "Snacks are in the bins." She pointed to a stack of white bins full of more snacks than we should need.

We also had a massive first-aid kit.

"Then we can head over," she said as she headed for her truck. That was what the trailer was attached to.

The kids were arriving at the stadium in a few hours, which gave us enough time to get everything set up. The plan was to have two kids to a tent and they'd be bringing their own sleeping bags. Which meant we needed to get ten tents set up. These were not the kind that would need to be nailed into the ground. There were rules with the field and we were going to respect every single one so that another group of kids would hopefully get to do this next year.

Urban had called every night after his game. He was adamant that he wasn't going to miss a single one since the last time he'd done that, it had disappointed both of us. Though I'd told him he didn't have to do that. He didn't owe me anything.

Each time, he'd scowled and at some point, I was going to have to be honest with myself when it came to him.

I just couldn't believe I was letting myself care about someone. Again.

But I'd fight it every step of the way because I just couldn't do it again.

"Everly!" Camden squealed when I got out of my car half an hour later. There were already some guys helping Lucia get the trailer unpacked. That suited me fine, given that I wasn't exactly looking forward to lugging all that down all the stairs.

But the guys had a huge cart that they were loading things onto.

"They'll take it down the elevator," Camden added when she saw me watching them.

"Perfect."

Camden looped her arm through mine to lead us into the stadium. "Harlowe will be here after she's done working and Amity will be here as soon as they're back."

"What does Harlowe do? And 'they'? Back from where?" So many questions from that one sentence she'd said.

"Harlowe's parents own Cleats & Kegs. The bar down the street that the players love. But she runs it and may as well own it. Between you and me, she's saving up to buy it from them."

We started down the hallway that I was now familiar with. It'd lead to the clubhouse and it was what had taken us down to the field when I'd been with the kids.

"If that's what she wants, I hope it works out for her." Though owning a bar sounded like a nightmare to me.

"It is. I think her parents would just give it to her, but she wouldn't take it. She'd want to buy it so they'd have money to retire on."

"Makes sense." Then I waited to see if she'd answer my question about Amity.

"And Amity is with the team. She travels with them sometimes and they should be back soon."

"They come here?" Because I had no idea how this all worked.

Camden nodded as she pulled open the door to the outfield. The guys and Lucia were already down here. "They return here and then are released to go wherever they want. The guys have to travel with the team. There's no leaving until you're released, which is usually right away. Their cars are all in that parking garage over there." She pointed her thumb behind her back. "Except the ones whose significant others dropped them off."

"Got it." We stopped next to the pile of tents. "This is like a world within itself."

"It really is."

We spent the next hour setting the tents up in a circle. Not too close, but close enough. That way, we could contain them to the middle of the tents once it got dark. Lucia grabbed the iPad and headed up to the entrance where we'd told the parents to drop them off while Camden and I went to get dinner ready. Around the same time, Harlowe and Amity showed up.

There would be no roasting hotdogs or marshmallows at the park. We'd ordered pizza and plenty of drinks for them. This was all going to be set up in the courtyard, where there were tables for us to sit at. There was no way pizza was being taken onto the field.

The kids were talking so much, they were barely eating. The excitement was getting the better of them.

The four of us sat at a table that was situated in such a way that we could see all of the kids. Lucia was chatting with a couple of the stadium security guys to whom she'd offered pizza.

"You're with Urban?" Harlowe asked. She had her red hair lying softly around her face and was wearing a cute T-shirt with khaki shorts. Amity was in shorts and a T-shirt as well, but her auburn hair was in a braid lying over her shoulder.

"No, she's not," Camden answered for me quickly. When Harlowe was going to protest, she said, "I told you I *wished* she were. Not that she was."

An uncomfortable feeling washed over me. No one should be wanting me with Urban. Hell, no one should even know about him and me. Of course, his sister did because he'd reached out to Camden more than once.

"My mistake," Harlowe conceded, then she gave Camden a look that I couldn't decipher. "Camden won't date players at all."

Camden groaned. "She's telling the truth, but I really don't want to explain why in front of Silas's girlfriend." She pointed at Amity then me. "Or Urban's… friend."

That made me want to know even more.

"You've already made it clear why," Amity countered, but there was sadness to her tone that made me really want to know.

But perhaps another time would be better. I

respected that she didn't want to talk about that kind of thing here or with me, I was the same way, but that didn't change the fact that I wanted to know.

Soon after, the kids were finished eating and it was time to do the activities.

First, it was a behind-the-scenes tour where the kids got to see the things they wouldn't normally. Camden led this tour, which seemed appropriate, given that she'd basically grown up in this place. This kids also all thought it was amazing that she had four brothers who were major league players and, of course, the kids had heard of all of them.

For the first time, I got to step into the clubhouse as well. I'd been down here several times to meet up with Urban, but never inside.

The lockers were lined with a uniform inside each one. The team was away, so these had to be their home uniforms for tomorrow.

See? I was picking up some things.

While Camden explained what went on in the clubhouse, my phone rang. Urban's face filled most of the screen when I answered.

"You're back." I stepped away from the kids. Camden was showing them the shower room.

There was nothing mundane about anything as far as the kids were concerned.

"I am." He squinted and moved closer to the camera, as if trying to see something on my end. "Where are you?"

I smiled and moved my phone out a little so that it would show that I was standing in front of his locker. It hadn't been intentional but now I viewed it as a happy little accident.

"You're in the clubhouse?" he asked.

"Camden is doing a tour. Don't worry. None of them are touching anything."

He chuckled. "I'm not worried about that at all."

Then his sister came out of the shower area and said, "Let's keep moving, kids."

"I have to go," I told him. "The tour train is leaving and I really don't want to get lost down here."

"I'll find you."

Now I had to get off the phone for a completely different reason.

Sure. Urban saying he would find me was a perfectly friendly thing to do, but with him, there always seemed to be more behind it. Probably because he'd already told me that we could be more. Whether he said the words or not, he was telling me every time we talked in other ways.

"All right." He sighed when I didn't reply. "I'll see you soon."

There was no chance of me disagreeing with him because as much as I didn't want to admit it to myself, I wanted to see him. Wanted to hear how the road trip had gone. Just... wanted to be in his space.

After a last glance at his locker, I hurried to catch up with the group.

Once the tour was complete, the kids were going to have some free time to play catch in the outfield. There were strict instructions not to go into the infield, but they could run around out there. Camden had told me that the grounds crew would be on the field as soon as we packed up in the morning to make sure it was in the condition it needed to be for the game tomorrow night. I didn't know what that entailed, but it helped me relax and let the kids have fun.

They were only a few minutes into playing catch when I heard a few of them cheering. When I looked up, they had surrounded Silas and Urban.

I furrowed my brows and glanced over at the other women. They seemed as surprised as I was.

It wasn't until the kids settled back in to play catch together that Silas and Urban came our way.

"What're you doing here?" Amity asked once they were close enough.

"Decided to come camp out," Silas told her. "You know, we've never camped on the field, either." He looked at Camden and asked, "How in the hell did you get Mom to agree to this?"

"First." She held up a finger. "Watch your language. These are ten-year-olds. Second, I promised to use pop-up tents so nothing goes into the ground."

"Nice."

But Urban hadn't said a word. He waited until the others were chattering away and took two more steps toward me. "I'd kiss you," he said. "But…" Then he nodded toward the kids.

"Yeah, better you don't. What're you doing here? Did you know you were coming when you called me?"

"I did." He folded his arms under his chest. "It was Silas's idea, but he asked if I wanted to come with him."

"And you obviously did."

He narrowed his eyes to me, watching or taking

inventory of every small movement. "Are you annoyed by me being here?"

My eyes widened. "No. Not at all. I'm sorry if that was how it sounded."

Camden hopped over to us. "You know you and Silas are going to have to share a tent, right?"

Urban cringed. "Why?"

Now I smiled. "The kids. We have to keep things separate. Since we have one girl in camp, she gets her own. One tent will have three boys in it because of that. They're cousins, so they don't care."

Camden wrapped her arm around mine and smiled. "I'll share with Everly so you two can have mine."

The guys weren't that happy about it, but what could they expect? This was a camp outing. Nothing romantic was going to happen.

Boy, was I wrong.

Once the kids were settled for bed, Urban and I were on the field talking about his road trip. Some of it he'd already told me about and some he hadn't. Eventually, I lay back on the grass, looking up at the sky. The sound from the tents had died down, which meant the kids had finally started to fall asleep.

Urban lay beside me as we talked quietly into the night.

It was now impossible for me to deny that I had feelings for him.

The question was: Would I embrace those feelings to see where this went?

Or would I continue to ignore them in the name of protecting my heart?

CHAPTER 14
URBAN

The sun woke me up earlier than I wanted to be up. Though I supposed that was probably a good thing, given that parents were going to be showing up to get their kids in the not-too-distant future.

Everly had told me last night that they were giving the kids a quick breakfast of bagels and donuts and then the woman she worked with would make sure that the kids were picked up.

I'd slept in my jeans last night because there wasn't a chance in hell that I was changing in the tent with my brother. I didn't give a shit about him seeing me naked. That was something that happened all the time, but what I did care about was how fucking small the thing was. We were already almost lying on top of each other.

Everly had changed into cotton shorts and a T-shirt, which, I assumed, weren't her normal pajamas. Here at camp, with the kids, she probably wanted to be prepared.

The noise outside of the tents grew as more kids woke up and the harder the women tried to get them organized.

Through the thin nylon, I heard Everly giving directions. Lucia, the woman she worked with, was going to set up breakfast. While Everly, Camden, Amity, and Harlowe were each going to take a group of five to the restroom for them to get ready for the day.

"Why the fuck are they yelling?" Silas asked with his face buried in the sleeping bag.

I chuckled. "They're not. What's wrong with you?"

"Sleeping on the ground fucking sucks." He pushed the bag back so that he could sit up. "This better not fuck up my game tonight."

I held up my hands. "This was your idea."

"Yeah. I know. I thought Amity would think it's sweet. I'm not sweet very often—"

"Don't I know it."

He scowled at me. "And I thought she'd appreciate it."

"I think she did. They all probably did. The kids went nuts when we got here."

"Yeah." He smiled. "They did."

After a quick search of the area around me, I found my shirt and pulled it on. I'd packed other clothes, but I'd barely worn these yesterday, so I wasn't sure I'd change. I would hit the clubhouse to brush my teeth, though. We all kept shit like that down there.

I pushed out of the tent to see Everly walking away with her group. She had a small bag in her hand, as did all of the kids. This must've been what they'd put their toothbrushes and shit in. Camden, Harlowe, and Amity were all headed in separate directions.

"I'm going to the clubhouse," I told Silas when he stood up next to me.

"Me too."

It wasn't twenty minutes later, we were back, but the women with the kids weren't.

"They're in the concourse," Silas said. He was looking at his phone with a small grin on his face. "Breakfast."

I nodded then headed that way.

The kids were all full of energy as Harlow and Camden went around the tables, asking the kids if they wanted a bagel. Everly and Amity were doing the same thing with boxes of donuts. On a table right behind them, there were a few other boxes. Then the women came to stop in front of Silas and me.

"Donut?" Amity asked.

"Or bagel?" Camden added. "Or both? Whatever. I really don't care what you eat."

Everly chuckled quietly. The sound made me want to smile.

"I'm good," I told both of them. What I didn't say was that I had another idea for breakfast.

The women hurried the kids because their parents were going to start picking them up. They started taking the kids in groups back to the field to get their regular bags then dropped them off with Lucia at the gate designated for pickup. Finally, we were on the field with no kids.

Everly huffed out a breath and put her hands on her hips. "Time to break all these tents down." I wasn't sure she was directly talking to me, but I didn't care. I was here and wouldn't stand there watching her work.

Amity and Silas got busy on a tent, as did Camden and Harlow. So I pointed to the one closest to where I was standing and Everly nodded.

"You don't have to help with this," she said as we flattened the tent. "Don't you have game stuff to do?"

"Not for a while. I don't mind helping." Then I took a breath. Asking Everly to breakfast shouldn't have made me feel like a middle schooler asking my first crush to dance. Yet here I was, a little worried. Not about asking. About Everly saying *no*.

It wasn't rejection I was worried about. It was her preferring we keep hiding behind closed doors.

Once we'd gotten the tent back into the sleeve it had come in, I asked, "How about we get breakfast after this?"

Her gaze locked with mine and it looked like she was trying to decide what the right thing to do was. I could've answered that for her. *Go with me.* That was the right thing.

"I don't know."

I furrowed my brows. "Are you not hungry?"

Her stomach made a noise as if on cue, and I raised an eyebrow while fighting a grin. The smell of the baseball field surrounded us. It was one of my favorite things. The only thing that could ruin this moment was for her to say *no*.

"You can hear that I am," she said. "But it's… public. Too peopley."

I took a step closer and lowered my voice. "Are you embarrassed to be seen with me?"

She shoved me without much effort behind it. "It's not that and you know it. I just… people will get the wrong idea and it seems like you'd be pretty recognizable."

I sighed. "It's just breakfast. You'd get breakfast with Camden, right?"

"You want to get breakfast with me?" Camden was suddenly by my side.

"No." My response was immediate.

"I just heard—"

"It was an example, Camden. I'm trying to get Everly to go to breakfast with me, and if it's something she'd do with you, then it's a friend thing, so there's no reason she shouldn't say *yes*." I looked back at her. "Unless she doesn't want to go."

Everly's chest deflated, like she'd taken a deep breath and was using the time to blow it out to stall giving me an answer.

"Fine," she finally said. "I'll go, but it's a bad idea."

Camden squinted up at me. "So we're all getting breakfast?"

I sighed. "No." Then I gave her a shove that was only hard enough to make her move a single step. She laughed loudly the entire time.

Finally, the tents were all packed into their carrying cases and loaded back into the trailer for Lucia to take back to camp.

"Where do you want to meet?" Everly asked.

"I'll drive us."

She shook her head. "I have my car here, so you'd have to bring me back and I know you probably have things to do before the game tonight."

I narrowed my eyes. It was only nine by this time. "There's a long time before the game tonight."

Her jaw tightened. "I'll meet you, Urban. Where?"

I gave her the name of a diner-style restaurant not far from the field, and I wound up following close behind her to the place.

Something was off with her. I wasn't sure if it was the whole *strangers seeing us in public together* thing or what, but it was definitely there.

We took our seats and ordered drinks. I wanted a cup of coffee and a water. Everly ordered water and an orange juice. We didn't really start to talk until the drinks had arrived and we'd put in our food orders. I was doing an egg white omelet while Everly was getting scrambled eggs, bacon, and toast.

"So what's going on?" I asked after too long of a silence.

"What do you mean?" She was avoiding looking at me, so I waited until she did. Then she sighed. "This is going against everything I said I wanted out of… whatever this is between us."

"Breakfast?"

"Yes." She glanced around. Everly had her blonde hair in a ponytail, but the flecks of gold in her green eyes were on fire. It was like they got brighter with her emotions.

"You could've said *no*."

"I did. You pushed."

I had pushed a little, but I hadn't intended to make her feel pressured. "I was only making the point that you'd go to breakfast with a friend. You're the one that keeps mentioning us being friends. So are we? Or not?"

She clenched her teeth together. "I want to be."

"Then what's the fucking problem?"

She sat back and I was going to look over my

shoulder, but then our food appeared on the table. Once the waitress was done, Everly leaned back in.

"So it's breaking your rules to get breakfast with a friend?" I asked, nudging her a little more. This was something I was tired of dealing with, so we might as well have it out now.

"No. I don't have rules, Urban. I make decisions."

"And you decided to not date anyone before I came along. You're not going to go back on that, right?" I pressed. Her jaw clenched harder. "That's fine. That doesn't mean that I can't make sure you know that *I* want to date *you*." I leaned over the table a little so I could keep my voice down. "I wasn't looking for anyone when I came here. Fuck, my whole goal is to get the fuck out of here at the end of the season. But I like you, Everly. You don't want to date. Fine. You don't have to. I just wanted to make sure you knew that I wanted something more in case you ever change your mind."

"So, you're for sure about leaving Michigan at the end of the season?" She wasn't looking at me but at her eggs as if they were the most interesting thing in this room.

"Yeah. I don't want to be here now let alone long term. It's a family thing."

The smallest hint of a smile crossed Everly's face. "Now that, I can understand." She opened her mouth to say something then snapped up straight, closed her eyes then slowly opened them. I glanced around, trying to figure out what had caused such an abrupt change in her demeanor, but I didn't see anything obvious.

Until someone said, "Evie?"

A woman with hair a few shades darker than Everly's came rushing over to our table. The two of them had enough of a resemblance that they had to be related.

"Evie." She came to a stop beside us and set her hand on Everly's shoulder. "I can't believe I'm seeing you here." Then the woman slid her gaze over me. "I'm Ramona. Everly's sister." She reached a hand out for me to shake and I did. "And you are?"

"Urban." That was the only answer she was going to get, given how uncomfortable she was making Everly. I might not have known exactly why, but I knew Everly wanted to crawl out of her skin right now.

"This is the sister I don't talk to," Everly told me, still not saying a word to Ramona.

Sister she didn't talk to? That meant it was the

sister who'd slept with her boyfriend. No wonder my girl was uncomfortable.

"We talk." Ramona giggled uncomfortably. "We talk, Evie."

Finally, Everly looked up at her. "I haven't seen you in, like, eight months. We don't talk. Don't worry. That wasn't me being sad about not talking. In fact, it's been the best eight months of my life. I'll assume tomorrow starts the best hopefully *years* of my life."

"You don't have to be mean," her sister snapped.

Everly moved out of the booth. "I'm not being mean. I'm telling you what you already know. I don't want you to contact me."

Then she walked out of the restaurant.

I pulled my wallet quickly from my pocket and dropped some bills on the table. I didn't know how many I'd left and I didn't care. As long as it covered the food we hadn't even eaten, I was happy. Then, despite Ramona's protest, I hurried after Everly.

It took a second for me to figure out which way to go, but once I saw Everly slowly walking down the sidewalk, I ran after her, hoping to stop her before she got to her car. Then I slowed to a walk once I'd caught up.

"So that was your sister," I said.

Everly pinched the bridge of her nose. "Yup. Now you can see why my boyfriend wanted to fuck her."

I furrowed my brows. "What are you talking about?"

She stopped on the sidewalk and turned to me. "She's gorgeous."

"She sounded fake."

"What?"

"She sounded fake," I told her. "When she came up to you, her voice. She sounded like someone sounds when they're pretending everything is fine when it clearly isn't. Then she said you talk when I know you don't. It was all fake."

"You're right." She threw her hands in the air. "She's fake, but I don't think that particular boyfriend really cared."

I put my hands on her shoulders then lowered myself so that we were at eye level. "Look. He was an idiot. I'm not sure how anyone who was with you could even *think* about anyone else. We're not together, as you like to point out, and *I* don't think about anyone else."

Her green eyes widened slightly before she put

her mask back on. "You can't say that to me," she said. "This is supposed to be casual."

Yeah, well, now seemed like a good time to tell her. "I know. I thought I could be casual with you because I'm easy that way. Makes it easier to leave when I get traded. But it's been impossible not to fall for you."

Her shoulders slumped. This wasn't the news she'd wanted to hear, clearly.

"I can't be anything but casual with you." Her words felt like a fucking knife right into my gut. "I can't chance my heart getting broken again."

"I won't break your heart," I promised.

"How can you say that?" Her voice wavered. If I didn't know better, I'd have said that she was fighting back tears, given the glistening in her eyes. "How can you say that you won't break my heart when just minutes ago, you said that your only goal is to leave at the end of the season?"

Well… fuck. I had said that. "Goals can change."

She shook her head. "I don't want to change your plans. I'm too broken to give you what you want and you can't be casual. You're leaving at the end of the season but I don't want to leave Kalamazoo. I love my job. Love the kids. So that only leaves one option."

I swallowed hard. This was not how I'd seen today going at all. "To not see each other anymore."

She nodded then quickly swiped a finger under her eye. "Exactly."

Then she turned and walked away.

Well, fuck.

CHAPTER 15
EVERLY

There was something heavy sitting on my chest. It wasn't a heart attack because it was a metaphorical heaviness.

The last thing that I had wanted was to stop seeing Urban altogether. But why couldn't he just keep it casual? He was the first person since my last boyfriend whom I had wanted to see for more than just one night and I had deluded myself into thinking that we were really friends who sometimes had sex.

OK. Maybe not sometimes. Maybe often.

Now… we weren't even friends.

The Knights had only been home for three days and then they were going back out onto the road and were going to be gone seven. For the life of me, I'd never understand this schedule.

I might not have wanted to date Urban, but I also hadn't wanted him gone from my life completely.

I could do this. Yet not hearing from him after the game Friday, and then again on Saturday, when I'd known he'd been in Kalamazoo, sure as hell felt like a breakup. That was me being ridiculous given that you have to be with someone to break up and we weren't together at my insistence.

That weekend, I ignored everyone and everything. It wasn't until Monday at camp that I talked to another person.

"What happened?" Jade asked as soon as I'd gotten out of my car in the parking lot. Somehow, this woman made the camp T-shirt and khaki shorts look like high fashion. She was wearing wedge sandals, which was a clear sign that she didn't do the things outside like I did. Jade had both wrists full of bracelets that were probably far too expensive to get paint all over.

I guess those with money didn't think about things like that.

"What are you talking about?" I began my walk toward the main building.

"I texted and called all weekend. You didn't answer. I was going to ask if it was because you were naked with your hot baseball player, but looking at you right now, it's definitely something else." She stopped and pulled me to stop with her. "Family shit? Are they bugging you for money again?"

I took a deep breath. Jade had been there with me through everything. She was the one person to whom I could tell everything.

"No. I mean, yes. Always but I'm fresh out of fucks to give."

"Good. You don't need to support them."

"I know." I sighed. "Then I went to breakfast with Urban on Friday after the kids got picked up. Ramona was there. She came over to us."

The sound of disgust in Jade's throat told me exactly what she thought of that. "I can't believe she still has the nerve to try to talk to you."

"Yeah. Me, either."

Jade's brown eyes searched mine, as if she'd know exactly what was wrong if she just looked hard enough. She'd get her answer either way.

"Look, I don't want to talk about it right now, but Urban and I aren't… doing whatever it was we were doing."

"Dating," she said. "You were dating." I scowled, but it didn't deter her at all. "What happened?" she asked, then she immediately added, "Forget I asked. You said you don't want to talk about it right now, so we'll do it tonight. I'll bring dinner."

There was no sense in arguing with her. I wasn't going to win.

After work, I went right home to shower the outdoors off of me. I had my wet hair pulled up into a bun and put on the only Knights T-shirt I had that I'd bought to go to the camp game, along with some comfortable shorts. I probably should've examined why I'd put on the Knights T-shirt, but as the queen of denial, I wasn't going to.

Right after I'd finished getting dressed, there was a knock on my door then Jade glided through with a large bag in her hand. We usually never waited for someone to answer the door at either of our apartments.

"I got us Italian. Is that good for you?" she asked. "Pasta? Carbs? Breadsticks?"

I was very hungry, so I said, "Sounds delicious to me." It did sound delicious, but I wouldn't be eating much of it.

Though this place had my favorite salad, and Jade had ordered extra of those for leftovers to store in my refrigerator. Once we were settled at my coffee table and something was playing on the TV, though I didn't know what, she finally descended.

"So, tell me what happened."

There was no use fighting with her, so I obeyed. I told her about Urban and me the night before at the baseball field, then I told her about breakfast and my sister showing up.

"Aww," she said when I told her about him not thinking about anyone else. "Have you talked to him since?"

I shook my head. "He usually texts me after his games, but he hasn't."

"Have *you* texted him? You can text him first, ya know."

I bit into my bottom lip as my way of telling her I hadn't without saying the words.

She sighed and moved closer to me before putting an arm around my shoulders. "Everly, have you considered that maybe opening your heart up to him wouldn't be the worst thing in the world?"

"No." When she giggled, I continued. "I haven't considered it, Jade, because I wasn't even dating him and I feel fucking heartbroken over the fact that we aren't seeing each other anymore. Could you imagine how I'd feel when he *actually* broke my heart? If I allowed myself feelings for him?"

Jade grimaced but then took a deep breath. At least she had the decency to not mention the tears burning my eyes. "Hate to break it to you, babe, but you already have feelings for him. Otherwise, none of this would bother you."

I dropped my head back onto the couch, trapping her arm between my head and the cushion. "I know. But I really wanted us to be friends. He's easy to talk to."

"I'm serious, though, Everly. If that Bryson guy never wanted to see you, you wouldn't care."

"I'd celebrate, though I will say he hasn't reached out in a while." That didn't mean I'd let my guard down. "Camden told me that he and Urban almost got into a physical fight in the clubhouse, but she didn't have the details as to why."

"I'm sure it had something to do with you, but whatever it took, I'll be glad if that man disappears from your life."

"Me too."

I was able to breathe normally again. For a few

minutes, I was only taking very deep breaths to ensure that I wouldn't cry. Crying wasn't even my thing, so it made zero sense. As I thought about what Jade had said about it not being the worst thing in the world to have feelings, my eye caught the sad flowers on the dining table.

Urban had sent me those and now, they were wilting.

I knew the feeling.

Jade stayed later than she should have, but she didn't want to go home until she thought I was in a good place, and I loved her for it.

But as I lay in my bed that night staring up at the ceiling, Jade's words rang in my ears. I could text him first.

I didn't think I'd done that a single time since we'd met.

Friday outside of the restaurant, I'd let my fears get the best of me, which I didn't do too often. If you didn't count the whole *not having a boyfriend out of fear that he'd hurt me* thing. That was a valid fear that had been proven justified time and time again.

Plus, Urban didn't want to stay in Kalamazoo, so that meant at the end of the season, we'd be done anyway.

But the way we'd left it didn't sit well with me, either.

And I *could* text him first.

So once I worked up the courage, I tapped a message out on my phone. *Have your games gone well?*

Though I supposed I could've looked that up online. The problem being was that I'd have no idea what made a good game. Urban and Camden were the ones who told me if something was good or bad or if he felt like he hadn't done his job.

Stats alone meant nothing to me.

Is this you changing your mind?

I swallowed hard. *I haven't changed my mind. I'd still like to see you, tho.*

Adrenaline shot through me. Maybe that had been a dumb thing to say. Maybe he wouldn't care. Maybe I was sending mixed signals.

Maybe it didn't matter because he never replied.

Camden wasn't at camp that week. She'd told me that she was going to the away games, so she wouldn't have been. She'd even said that I should come with her, but that, I shot down for several reasons. The first being it would send mixed signals to Urban, especially now that we weren't seeing each other anymore. Second, it sounded expensive.

I didn't live the life that she did, or Urban did, or Jade did. It was different.

In my mind, even with my decent savings, I couldn't afford the week off work or the cost of the trip. You never knew when the next emergency would happen.

That made for a quiet week. Jade spent as much time with me as she could, but eventually, I had to kick her out. She had things to do and had even canceled going to an engagement party for friends of her family to hang out with me.

This was what I didn't want. I didn't want my heart to hurt and I didn't want my best friend taking care of me.

I knew when the team got back on Sunday night because Camden texted me demanding that I meet her at Cleats & Kegs, her best friend's bar near the ballpark. At first, my automatic answer was *no*. Then she said her brothers weren't there because her flight had landed earlier than theirs did.

That was when I decided to throw caution to the wind and meet Camden.

She was already in a booth near the bar when I arrived. This was more of a bar and grill vibe and they did have some food. It was the kind of place you could be comfortable without it being a dive bar. And it was busy without being packed. I hadn't done anything much to dress up. I was wearing shorts and a T-shirt. My hair was down, but only with a slight wave that formed naturally, and I hadn't put on any makeup.

"Hey." She smiled widely.

"You have got to be the happiest *after-traveling* person I've ever met." I dropped into the booth across from her. "Most people are ready for a nap when they land."

She laughed and looked wider awake than I did and all I'd done was lie around my apartment all day. "I think most people don't travel the way I did this week."

"What do you mean?"

"My parents had me take their private plane. I didn't have to wait with hordes of people."

Meaning, if I'd have gone, I probably wouldn't have had to buy plane tickets all week. Nah. I still wouldn't have gone, considering where Urban and I were.

"How did it go?" I asked because Camden could also explain what was good and what was bad.

"It was good. They won more than they lost.

The Knights are in first place, but it's still early in the season."

Right. It was June and Urban had told me that they played into September, October if they made the playoffs, which he thought they would.

What a long fucking season.

"That's good," I said, then a pop appeared in front of me.

"I pay attention," she told me. "You don't drink and always get a diet when you do order a pop, so I took the chance."

"Well, thank you." I took a nice, long drink. I didn't think I was obvious about the fact that I didn't drink, but either I was, or Camden paid close attention. It wasn't something I was embarrassed about, but most of the time, when a person said they didn't drink, it was followed by questions. Or that was my experience, anyway.

I never wanted to answer the questions.

"Urban played well," she offered, though I hadn't asked. "Angry, but well."

"What do you mean, *angry*?"

She shrugged. "I feel like he was looking for a fight with someone, and I don't necessarily mean with fists. The players yap back and forth all the time, and he was definitely trying to goad the other teams. Nothing big happened." She snorted. "Earlier this year, I was at the games in New York and my brother Cobb is on that team. Then Silas and Brooks were on the Knights. Urban hadn't been traded yet. Anyway, Silas ended up charging at the pitch, which turned into a full-out brawl with my brothers on opposite sides."

My eyes widened. "What happened?"

"Brooks held Cobb off. He's a pitcher and if he fucked up his hand, he probably wouldn't be able to play again. He's twenty-three and his career would be over."

"Yeah. That would suck."

"Anyway, nothing like that happened." She swirled her straw in her drink as I waited for what I knew was coming. "I figured that if Urban was in a shitty mood all week, that you might be too, so I wanted to check on you."

Shaking my head, I said, "You don't have to check on me, Camden. I'm fine. I'm sure your brother is fine. Someone probably irritated him is all." Yeah. Me.

Camden eyed me suspiciously. "Right. *Something* happened, anyway."

Luckily, I was able to change the subject so that we could spend the next half hour laughing about things at camp or something one of us had said. I liked Camden and hoped when things settled down with Urban that she wouldn't be put in the middle and not be my friend anymore. I didn't *think* that'd be the case.

As we laughed, the door opened and a bunch of loud guys came streaming in. It wasn't until the fourth face that I realized this was at least some of the Knights team. Brooks gave it away. He and Jenner were there, but Silas and Urban weren't.

Silas made sense. He probably wanted to spend the night at home with Amity.

Camden rolled her eyes. "They have an off day tomorrow, so a bunch of them end up here."

"I think I'm going to head out."

"Why?" She reached out and put her hand on mine. "Urban isn't going to come. He's probably still in a bad mood."

They'd had a day game today and then flown home. It was barely seven-thirty, and suddenly, my stomach reminded me that I was hungry. But there was something else I needed to do first.

I shook my head. "That's not why. I just want to curl up in my pajamas with some ice cream." Which would be exactly what I did after I took care of something else.

"All right, but let's go shopping or something soon."

"Absolutely." Though I didn't love shopping, if Camden wanted to go, I'd go with her. It was the same way that I often humored Jade.

I had to push my way through the Knights crowd and was thankful when I got outside. After getting into my car and hitting the locks—a woman should never sit in a parked car without locking the doors—I pulled my phone out of my purse and hit his contact without hesitation. If I hesitated, I'd chicken out.

Urban answered on the third ring. "Hello?"

I opened my mouth, yet nothing came out. He sighed.

"Everly?"

"Can I come over?" I asked quickly so he wouldn't hang up.

"*What?*"

"Can I come over to talk to you?"

"I haven't changed my mind, Everly. If you don't want to be with me, that's fine, but—"

With a quieter voice, I said, "Can I come over?"

He sighed, then said, "Sure. Come over."

It took maybe fifteen minutes for me to get to his apartment, but another three to get me to knock on the door. When I finally did, he opened it right away, like he'd just been waiting for me to knock.

Nervous butterflies took off in my stomach as if their lives depended on it, but I knew I couldn't let that scare me off.

I needed to talk to him.

CHAPTER 16
URBAN

"What're you doing here?" I asked, pressing one hand on the door and the other on the jamb the way a person would if they were letting someone know she wasn't coming in.

I hadn't seen—or talked—to her in a week. My eyes were starved for the sight of her. She was wearing shorts and a T-shirt. Her hair was down with a slight wave and all I wanted was for it to be OK for me to fist my hand in it.

But it wasn't.

Now, I'd just gotten comfortable when she called, so I was standing before her in jeans and a white T-shirt. My feet were bare, hair tousled. I'd cracked a beer since we didn't have a game tomorrow.

"Can I…?" Everly blew out a breath that made her bangs dance across her forehead. "Can I come in?"

I moved my arm and stepped back so that she'd come into my apartment. As fucking pissed as I was, seeing her still did something to my chest. Turned it into jelly. A quickly hardening jelly, but jelly nonetheless.

Everly swallowed hard and shifted her weight like she was nervous. "Your sister said you were in a bad mood all week."

I snorted. "Wonder why."

She took another breath. "I was also told that you almost came to blows with Bryson." She closed her eyes for longer than a blink then opened them again. "Was that about me?"

I loosened my arms and wet my bottom lip. I could've lied, but what would be the point of that? "Yeah."

"Because he and I slept together?"

I backed up until my ass leaned against the back of the couch. "No. Do I love that he's seen you naked? Not really. But no, that wasn't why."

"Barely," she whispered. When I furrowed my

brows, she continued. "We didn't get completely undressed and—"

My hand flew up before I knew what was happening. "Nope. I have exactly zero desire to hear any of this. I hate all of it. I don't need you to have been a virgin before me, but I don't need to hear about you with someone else."

Maybe I'd said it a little too harshly.

She snapped her mouth shut. "Then why?"

I worked my tense jaw back and forth. Why the fuck did she want to know? Why was she here, other than to check on me and my shitty attitude, which she didn't have a reason to do anymore? We couldn't be together because that was what *she* wanted. We couldn't be friends because I didn't think I could do that.

Friends met boyfriends—or casual whatevers since she refused to have a boyfriend—and as much as I'd like to think I was evolved, I knew better. I couldn't stand there and watch her be with someone else when I wanted her so badly, I could taste it.

But I also might as well tell her the truth. "He said something shitty about you and I didn't like it."

She closed her eyes again and swallowed hard. "I can imagine."

"I honestly hope the fuck you can't."

Suddenly, Everly was looking everywhere, but at me when she asked, "Are you mad at me? It's a dumb question, I know. And normally, I don't give a shit if a hookup is mad at me, but—"

I stood to my full height then walked over to the bottle of beer I'd left on the table, taking a nice long drink. "You really need to stop referring to me as a 'hookup.' You might not want to admit it, but it was more than friends who have sex." I shrugged. "At least it was to me."

"No. I know it was," she said quietly.

"Do you want a drink?" I asked because it didn't seem like she was going anywhere anytime soon. I sure as hell wasn't going to ask her to leave. At least not yet.

"I'll take some water."

Everly didn't drink. She'd never said there was a reason for it, but she didn't. Not even a sip in the weeks that I'd known her. Now maybe she did sometimes and I just didn't know about it, but everything told me that she fully abstained.

After getting her a glass of water, I took it out, walked past her, and set it on the coffee table. "May as well sit down. I don't think you're going anywhere."

Everly pushed off her shoes then came over to sit on the couch. She folded one leg under her and as much as I wanted to sit as close as possible to her, I sat on the other end. She didn't want me close—that meant I wouldn't be close.

"Do you want me to leave?" she asked after taking a drink of her water. She clutched the glass, like she was afraid it was going to run away.

"No," I told her honestly. "If I had my way, you'd be here a lot, but I don't get my way, do I?"

Everly swallowed hard and took a deep breath. "What would that look like?"

"What?"

"Us. Together. What would that look like?" Her gaze finally met mine. "Think about it realistically, Urban. You travel a ton. I have to work as much as possible all the time." She bit into her bottom lip again. That had to be a nervous habit. "You're leaving at the end of the season."

I leaned over to set my bottle on the table then turned to her fully.

"What would that look like?" I asked her, but I didn't wait for an answer. "It'd look like you're mine and I'm yours. We'd be together. It'd look like… yeah. I have to travel. I'd try to convince you to come every single time. Not with me on the team bus or plane because that isn't allowed, but to come. We'd get to spend time together."

"You'd want me to stay at the hotel with you?"

"Fuck yes, but you can't. It's part of the team rules. You wouldn't even be able to stay at the same hotel."

She furrowed her brows. "I'd never be able to afford that lifestyle, Urban. I'd never be able to go."

Well… that was confusing. As if I'd have her pay. "You honestly think I'd have you pay for your own trip when the only reason you were going was because of me? Fuck that."

She winced and I knew she hated the idea of me paying for something like that.

It had to be her fucking family.

"I don't take money from other people," she said quietly. "I promised myself a long time ago that I wouldn't be like my family. I wouldn't be a financial burden on someone else."

I snorted. "'Burden.' Baby, do you know how much I make a year? I wouldn't even notice."

"What else?" she asked, clearly done with the topic of money.

If she was going to give me the chance to convince her, I was going to take it. But I'd be careful because Everly would run. There was no doubt of that.

"I know you have to work. I'd try really fucking hard not to interfere. Most of the school year, I'm here. Or whatever city my team is in. In the off-season, I mostly just work out a shit ton and sometimes I'll hit batting cages and shit like that. But I'm not nearly as busy October to mid-February."

"Four months?" she asked.

"Yeah." I nodded. "I know the schedule sucks, but I'm doing something I love and it's not forever. There are a limited number of years I can play."

"But you're leaving at the end of the year."

That was the sticking point. I could see it in her eyes. She thought I'd make her fall in love with me then just leave. *Fuck.* Maybe I should've kept my mouth shut. I slipped across the couch until I could lay my arm along the back of it, which created a little cocoon between the two of us.

"When I came here, all I could think about is leave. I can't lie about that. I never wanted to play for Kalamazoo strictly because of my dad. There wasn't anything here for me, really." I ran my thumb over her cheekbone. "Things change."

"You could still get traded." That was a sticking

point for her and it was up to me to convince her that it wouldn't matter.

"If I got traded, I'd want you to come with me." Her eyes widened and her mouth opened. "You probably wouldn't be able to, but I'd want you to. Since you couldn't, we'd figure it out. Not to mention, me being traded is almost impossible if I don't push for it. My mom wants me here and she's the one who makes the decisions. But if I want you to come with me now, how do you think I'll feel at the end of the season?"

She snorted. "Sick of me, probably."

"Not possible."

"You can't break my heart, Urban. I don't think I can do it again." Her eyes shimmered in the light, like she was holding back tears.

Her fear was real. Some people would say that she just needed to get over it, but those people weren't looking into her eyes and seeing the hurt. It made me rage inside. How could anyone look at this woman and hurt her?

"I won't," I promised. "I won't do anything to hurt you, Everly. And I've met your sister. Even if she weren't your sister, I wouldn't fuck her."

She laughed for the first time she'd gotten here and to see her smile tugged at my heart. "Good to know," she said. Everly wiped under both of her eyes, though as far as I could tell, she hadn't shed a tear. "OK. We have to pace ourselves, though, OK? The way you're talking, it sounds like you're five minutes away from declaring your love for me or something." A smile played on her lips. If only she knew how close to the truth that was. "I'm not sure I could handle that yet."

I shrugged. "I'll wait for you to say it first." Seemed like the best compromise. Didn't mean I wouldn't shower her with my feelings every single day as they grew. And there was no doubt that they would grow.

"How about some food?" She pushed to her feet. "Let's get dinner. I'll buy."

I was about to protest, but she raised her eyebrow in a challenge, so I snapped my mouth closed. If she needed to pay for dinner, I'd let her without any complaints from me.

Everly chose the place and drove, as well. She took me to Cleats & Kegs, where half my damn team was. Which meant I was stopped almost as soon as I got in the door. Jenner and Brooks tried dragging me toward their table, but I pushed them off. I wasn't here to hang out with them. I was here to have dinner with my girl.

It was just surprising that she'd chosen a place she had to know would be packed with ballplayers. And people who loved to chase after ballplayers. Before, she hadn't wanted to be seen in public with me, but she couldn't really get more public than this right now.

Once we were in a booth on the far side of the room away from my coworkers, I looked at her expectantly. At first, she ignored it. Then she sighed.

"I really like their burgers." She shrugged.

"Yeah." I leaned my elbows on the table and folded my hands in front of my face. "They have great burgers here."

As hard as she tried, she couldn't stop the smile that she battled so valiantly not to show. "Fine. I figured, rip off the Band-Aid. I was here earlier with Camden and knew the team was here." She glanced over at the large table in the middle of the place that was absolutely packed with the guys. "Or most of them. Silas wasn't here."

"He wouldn't be. He'd be home with Amity."

"Anyway. I figured you weren't going to go along with the whole *keeping a low profile* thing. Staying out of the public eye so people wouldn't see us together and think we're together."

"You're right. I wouldn't. Because we *are* together."

She rolled her beautiful, green eyes. "I know. I don't have to be reminded. But I figured why not let them all make their assumptions now? You don't have a game tomorrow. I have to work and you do have your volunteer time at camp tomorrow. So, I brought us here."

"Trust me." I reached across the table to take her hand in mine. "I don't mind at all. This is the last week of camp, isn't it?"

She nodded. "It's the last for this group. There will be another baseball unit for a different group of kids in a few weeks, but that also means different volunteers." A cloud moved over me. Everly must've noticed, given that she immediately said, "Camden made sure the volunteer list is exclusive."

"I knew I liked my sister."

With all of that behind us, we were able to enjoy a casual dinner in a very crowded bar and grill.

When we got back to my apartment, I didn't even have to ask her to come in. She just got out of the car, put her hand in mine and let me take her inside. After I got the door open, I hit some light switches so we wouldn't be in complete darkness.

"You don't have to be surprised that I came in with you," she told me as she pushed her shoes off. "I *do* know how to behave in a relationship. The guys usually don't."

I chuckled. "I don't know if I'm the best, but I know I won't hurt you."

"I hope not," she said quietly and she turned to me, those green eyes making me hard just by looking at me. "You don't have to keep reassuring me about it. I'm going to trust that you won't."

"Good." I put my hands on her hips and pulled her into me.

Everly craned her neck so that she could see me. I towered over her, but not so much that it was ridiculous. "What scares me most about you, Urban, is that my feelings are already too big. I already care too much. I already want too much."

"What's 'too much'?" I asked, but it was rhetorical. That was my way of telling her that *too much* didn't exist as far as I was concerned.

Before she could respond in any way, I pushed my lips against hers gently, showing her how much care I'd take with her. Everly pushed her fingers into my hair and squeezed, lighting me on fire.

Because no matter what, I'd be gentle with my wounded girl.

CHAPTER 17
EVERLY

Urban's mouth on me felt better than anything else.

We'd had sex several times, but that had always been a fast push toward our releases. That wasn't to say we hadn't taken our time to make sure we'd both gotten to where we'd needed to be. But this felt different.

The two of us were standing just inside his front door. His hand slid around my neck until he could grasp the back of it. And hold on tight he did. His mouth was so gentle while his tongue was demanding. I'd give whatever he wanted to take.

I slid my hands up his chest until I reached his shoulders. As he kissed me, I used the leverage to jump. He caught me under the ass as I wrapped my legs around his waist. Then we were moving. To the bedroom, I assumed, but I didn't open my eyes, instead choosing to trust him.

That was what this whole thing was about, anyway. Trust. I'd do it until he gave me a reason not to, but my heart was so guarded, it wouldn't take much to break that trust.

Instead of focusing on what might go wrong, I decided I'd focus on the beautiful man before me.

Urban set me on the bed on my knees. I could still reach to pull at his shirt. That was when he finally broke away from me so he could yank that white T-shirt over his head. Then my shirt went. And my bra.

He kissed down my neck, over my collarbone, then over the swell of my breast before licking my nipple and taking it into his mouth. My head dropped back and I moaned as he scraped his teeth over it. I was so sensitive, so ready, so fucking needy for him.

I didn't think I'd ever been this needy for anyone in my life, and I was determined not to be afraid of it.

Urban slipped his hands into the back of my shorts and squeezed my ass while I let my fingers walk slowly down his chest and abdomen until reaching the button on his pants. There was something about this moment. I wanted him inside me.

Finally, though not quick enough for me, we were both naked. I moved off the bed and pointed to it. "Lie down," I told him.

He furrowed his brows but did what I'd instructed.

"Condom?" I asked.

"Wouldn't you rather use your own?"

A moment of pause went through me like ice water in my veins. He was right. I always carried some with me for moments like this, but right now… there weren't any in my purse.

"Trust, right?" I asked. His thick cock jumped and hit his belly lightly.

"Right here." He slid open the nightstand drawer and pulled a condom out.

When he went to rip it open, I lunged and slapped his hand away. "I'll do it," I told him.

He lay back, letting his hands fall against the pillow. The moment I touched him, his eyes darkened. As quickly as I could, I slid the condom down then climbed on top of him and impaled myself on his cock. He grabbed my hips tightly.

"Everly," he rasped out. "You didn't—"

"I will."

Every time we'd been together, Urban had given me an orgasm before we'd gotten here. Today, *I* was in control.

"I needed you inside of me," I told him.

Air sucked in between his teeth, but his grip loosed just a little. This was his way of making sure he didn't try to control my actions.

I pushed my hips forward and back. Since I was sitting up straight, I wouldn't have been able to take another inch of him. I was as full as I could be. Urban's hands roamed my body. He cupped my breasts, his thumbs running over my hard nipples.

Though I was ready to stay right here, suddenly, Urban pulled out, flipped me over onto my back, and slammed into me. My head fell back.

Fuck, that felt good.

He made just enough room to reach his hand between us and press against my clit. He didn't have to do it too many times before my legs clamped down on his hips. It did nothing to stop him. Once I'd met my release, he followed right after.

It would take a minute for me to catch my breath.

"Shit," I said. It sounded like I'd just run a four-minute mile. Something I absolutely couldn't do.

"No kidding." At least he sounded winded too. "Sorry I took over. Couldn't help it."

A slow grin formed on my lips. "I don't mind at all."

He reached over, cupping my cheek, and kissed me again. This was slow and deep. There was so much behind it that I had to remind myself he'd said he was going to wait for me before declaring anything.

But I kind of felt like he just had.

"You should use the bathroom first," he told me. My skin felt warm all over, and there were some muscles that would be sore tomorrow, especially in my legs.

"Why?"

He rolled to his side and pushed some of my hair off my shoulder before kissing my left breast softly. "Because I don't want to come out of there with you dressed and ready to leave."

I snorted. That was my fault. "I'll go first." I pushed off the mattress and swung my legs over the side. "But I can always get dressed after."

He closed his eyes and groaned so he didn't see me snag his T-shirt off the floor as I made my way to the bathroom. When I came out, Urban was still lying on the top of his blanket, completely naked, with his arms folded behind his head. His T-shirt hung to my mid-thigh and was loose. Perfectly comfortable to sleep in.

"Well, I like the look of that," he told me as he watched me cross the room and climb up onto his bed.

He reached over to pull me into him, but I didn't let him. "Ew. No. Gross. You have a used condom hanging off you." Then I used both hands to push him. He barely moved. "Go take care of it."

Urban swung his legs off the bed, then stopped and turned to me. It didn't take much to know exactly what he was thinking.

"I'll be here when you get back," I assured him. Those times that I'd basically kicked him out or when I'd left his apartment had left their mark.

I wouldn't have said he was scared. It was concern I'd seen on him.

So after pulling my panties back on, I yanked his blanket and top sheet back and settled myself into his cloud from the sky. Seriously. That was the only explanation as to why his bed was so damn comfortable.

Or wait… this wasn't his bed, was it?

My mind started to run with several scenarios of what others had gotten up to in this very place, but thankfully, Urban came out before I could get too far.

He snatched his boxer briefs off the floor, pulled them on, then climbed in beside me. After he wrapped his arms around me tightly with his cheek to my back, he kissed the side of my head. His arms were like pillars of steel holding me to the bed, and there wasn't anywhere else I'd rather be right now.

Surprisingly, I was able to keep any panic away. I believed it when Urban said he wouldn't hurt me, but I didn't think two of the three previous douchebags had intended to hurt me from the get-go. For them, it had been more that temptation had presented itself, and they couldn't fight it. Still made them douchebags, of course.

But who had more temptation than Urban Briggs? Other than his fellow teammates.

No. That was something I was going to have to deal with. Unfortunately for him, that meant I'd probably spook at the first sign of something shady.

Maybe I shouldn't say *unfortunately for him*, given that he shouldn't be doing anything that would make me second-guess what he was doing.

At least those thoughts didn't haunt me all night and I was able to fall asleep relatively easily. Even if it was in his bed. A place I'd sworn I'd never be for more than a romp.

My body had an internal clock that woke me early enough to get home and ready for camp without being late.

I was putting my shoes on by the door when Urban walked out in his boxer briefs with his hair messy from sleep.

"Where are you going?" His voice was deep and it sounded like he'd run sandpaper lightly over it. A sexy sound that would likely go away after his first drink of water.

"Home."

He scowled and came to a stop right in front of me. So close that if I moved too quickly, I'd fall backward into the door.

"What?" I asked.

"I thought you weren't going anywhere." His jaw tightened and as sexy as this man was first thing in the morning, I didn't want him looking at me that way.

"I said that last night."

"Exactly. It's fucking early and you're sneaking out." He put his hands on his hips, like he was expecting me to fight him on that.

I wouldn't because I *was* leaving. "Yeah," I told

him. "To go home and change then go to work. Some of us work fucking early."

All that tension left his face, only to be replaced with regret. "I'm sorry," he said. "I thought you were sneaking out."

I placed each of my hands on an arm and squeezed. "I told you I wasn't going to do that. You're going to have to trust that the way I have to trust that you're not going to break my heart."

"You're right." He wrapped his arms around my back and pulled me to him. His body was still warm from sleep. "I am. I shouldn't have assumed."

"No, you shouldn't." I sighed and leaned my head against his chest. Suddenly, I was surrounded by the smell of Urban. I didn't know if it was his soap, his location, or just him, but it was definitely Urban. A cross between summer and Earth.

I was getting so fucking weird.

"But," I continued as I pulled away, "I am the one who gave you reason to think that I'd ditch you after sex like that, so I'll just have to prove to you I won't from now on."

"So work?" he asked as I put on my other shoe. "Why not play hooky?"

I scrunched up my face at him. "Several reasons, actually. It'd be irresponsible of me to call in, and I like this job. Your family might not like me calling in to hang out with you. Not to mention, you have to be at camp today, too."

He chuckled. "I promise they won't fire you."

"You can't make that promise."

He cocked his head to the side and smirked. "I think I can."

I shook my head then pushed up onto my toes to give him a quick kiss. "I don't want you pulling any strings."

"All right. After, then?"

Definitely after.

And that was how it went. I headed off to work that day then met him after. This time, I planned to stay at his apartment. We didn't go out. When he didn't have a game, we were there on his couch, eating whatever takeout we'd gotten that day, or if I happened to cook, talking about all things we were supposed to talk about.

But we avoided the topic of him leaving at the end of the summer because with each passing day, I didn't want to think about it. Sure, Urban said he was already changing his mind, that didn't mean his mind was changed.

Each day he had a game, I met Camden or Amity and went to the ballpark. I was actually learning a few things and could see the appeal of the sport, even if I wasn't ever going to be a die-hard fan.

Die hard for Urban, but probably never the game.

Unfortunately, the week passed quickly and they were headed out onto the road. He stayed at my apartment the night before he left. Already had his bag in the car. I thought about asking if I should take him to the stadium, but I didn't want any public goodbye. Not like he was going off to war or anything. This was going to be the first night we were spending apart since deciding to be together.

It'd be weird.

It was surprising how quickly I'd gotten used to sharing a bed with him.

"I'll let you know when we get there," he told me. For a guy who hadn't done the girlfriend thing in a while, he was pretty good at it.

"And call after the games so you can tell me what was good and bad," I said. He snorted while I shook my head at him. "It's the only way I'm going to learn."

"Yeah. After the game, too."

When he kissed me goodbye, his hand cupped my ass and lifted so that I'd have no choice but to wrap my legs around his waist. Then I hugged him with everything I had, hoping it'd be enough to remind him that he had someone back home who lo—cared about him.

Camden again had wanted me to come—at least for part of the trip. But there was no way. I had work. She reminded me that I could request days off. It wasn't like I was an indentured servant, but alas, I was going to work. This was too short of notice to take off.

She told me I was going on one of the road trips, and somehow, it sounded like a thinly veiled threat.

It was the second night of the road trip and the Knights were playing in Charlotte. It seemed to be going as normal. Of course, what did I know about baseball? Instead of a commercial break, one of the sports casters was on the screen. He was standing at the ballpark where Urban was playing.

"Sad news out of Knights nation." Which was what I'd learned the fans and entire organization was lovingly referred to as. "The Knight's owner, Silas Whitlock, current GM AnnMarie Briggs's father, has had a stroke." I slapped a hand over my mouth. "There's not much information on the eighty-two-year-old's current condition, but we do know he's under the care of the best doctors. We'll keep you up to date as we learn more."

The camera flashed to one of the guys who announced the game. I couldn't remember his name right then if my life depended on it. "What does that mean for tonight's game?" he asked.

As if that mattered.

The camera went back to the original guy. "I'm told that all three of the Briggs on the team have been notified. They've decided to finish the game and head back to Michigan after it's done."

The regular announcer said, "Our thoughts will be with the family through this difficult time."

And then they just cut back to the regular commercial, as if nothing else had happened.

At first, I sat there. I couldn't call Urban. He was on the field somewhere. So I did the next best thing.

I grabbed my phone so quickly that I almost dropped it. Once I had it in hand, I chose Camden's contact. She'd know what was going on.

"Hello," she said, sounding out of breath. Last I'd known, she'd been at the game, but it sure didn't sound like it.

"Camden, how are you? How is your grandpa?"

She sighed. "He's… I don't know. They don't really know yet. Just that he had a stroke."

"I'm watching the game and they just announced it. Are you there? The guys are still playing?"

A door in the background shut and I heard voices behind her. It didn't sound like a game at all. "I'm here. In Kalamazoo. I came back last night because Grandpa wasn't feeling good and Mom was going over there. I wanted to go too." Her voice sounded watery, like she had just been crying or was about to start. Then she blew a breath against the phone. "The guys know. They decided to finish the game, then they'll head back here. It's a short flight and this gives Mom the time to get the jet there so they won't have to fly commercial and deal with that."

"Are they… OK? Are you?" When I glanced at the screen, the game was back and the camera zoomed in on each of the Briggs' faces. They were hard, stoic—looked like they always did during a game. "They're on TV now and they look… the same."

"Yeah, well, baseball players spend years learning how not to show emotion. That way, the other team doesn't see a weakness. They're coming back on bereavement, so they'll be here a few days."

My stomach turned. I knew that as much as Urban didn't like his father, he loved his grandpa. "Isn't that just for… a death?"

"No. They can take it for illness. Listen, the doctor is talking to Mom, so I'm going to go. I'll text you when I know more."

Then the line went dead.

Maybe once I knew when they were coming, I could pick the guys up at the airport or something.

All I knew was that I couldn't just sit here twiddling my thumbs.

CHAPTER 18
URBAN

Of all the fucking things to find out in the middle of a game. My grandpa had had a stroke. They don't know how bad it was, but we should probably get back to Kalamazoo as soon as we could.

We were told they could pull us, but none of us would leave the game. Leaving something unfinished wasn't how we did things.

So we played. We won. I got a home run and figured that was for Grandpa. He fucking loved this game, and he would've smacked us on the backs of our heads if we'd left in the middle. But he would be proud as hell for us staying.

Once the game was over, Brooks, Silas, and I ran for the clubhouse, showered off as quickly as we could, then grabbed our bags and headed for the car that our coach had told us would be waiting for us.

The first thing I wanted to do was call Everly. The way I was ready to crawl out of my skin made me worried that I'd scare her. Did she even know what had happened?

Maybe it was better to wait until I was actually in Kalamazoo. That way, I could get to her. She didn't know my grandpa, but she knew me, and she'd be able to hear the worry in my voice, which would worry her.

No. I'd wait.

Amity wasn't on this trip, so Silas could meet up with her in Kalamazoo when we got there.

Then my sister sent a text saying there'd be a car at the airport, and that was it. Not who to look for or if she'd rented us something. At least she finally responded that it'd be a car with a driver, and since we were flying into the private hangar, it'd be right there waiting for us. No searching.

One less thing to worry about.

The time on the plane gave me too long to think.

"You know, maybe we've all spent too much

time being pissed at Dad," Brooks said. Apparently, I wasn't the only one thinking it.

"He was a fucker when we little," Silas told him, as if we didn't all know that.

"He was," Brooks said. No one could deny that. "But I've always felt that it was because he cared. Not just to be an asshole. More like he had not idea how to feel what he felt."

"I agree." I met Brooks's gaze. "But he *was* an asshole."

"Yeah."

"I get what you're saying, though," I told him because it was what I'd just been thinking too. "That maybe it's time to get over all that shit."

Silas cocked his head to the side. "Is this because there's another reason you want to stay at the end of summer?"

I shook my head. "I never said I wanted to stay."

"You don't have to," Brooks countered. "We're your brothers. Older, at that, and we've known you every single minute of your life. You don't have to say it."

"But you shouldn't deny it," Silas added. "If you love that girl, there's no reason to."

"I didn't deny it," I told them. "I actually didn't say fuck all about her."

"So you'd leave?" Brooks asked. "Knowing that she's here?"

"I didn't say that, either. Right now, I'm focused on Grandpa and why the fuck this plane doesn't go faster."

Brooks furrowed his brows. "It's going, like, four hundred miles per hour. That's pretty fast."

Yeah. My knee started to bounce, though I hadn't intended it to. It was just all this energy I had inside of me with no place to go. I'd just played an entire game. It should have been gone, but when something I cared about was in harm's way, it was like I had an endless amount just waiting to be used.

"What made you think about Dad?" Silas asked Brooks as he moved his armrest up and down. Looked like I wasn't the only one with energy to spare.

"I don't know," he said as he sat back. "Thinking about Grandpa… it's not going to be that long before we're in this position with Mom and Dad. Fuck. It could happen any day because bad shit happens. Look at Amity's brother. No one expected that."

A cloud moved over Silas' face at the reminder

of something he thought he was responsible for. He hadn't been but that didn't stop the guilt.

"Dad's going to a nursing home," I told them to lighten the mood. "But seriously, my main goal was anywhere but here so I wouldn't have to deal with him. That means I've been gone a lot, and sure, I came back and got to see Grandpa, but it's not like it is with Brooks. Or even you since you've been back a while. I missed a lot of time just because I wanted to avoid the head fucker."

Brooks sighed. "I'll tell you the secret. And I'll tell Cobb since I'm sure he's on the way home right now, too. If you just learn what's worth arguing about with that man and what isn't, life gets easier."

"We've been doing that since we were fifteen."

He shook his head. "No. Not like that. We're grown men. He wants to spew his advice and shit, but he has no control over what we do. He doesn't have a hand in the team, so fuck him."

"Maybe after this, we'll have a sit-down with him and lay all this shit out once and for all," Silas suggested. He grinned widely. "Do you think we could get Cobb to play here then?"

"No," Brooks and I said at the same time, then we chuckled. Poor Cobb was the youngest of the boys. Which meant he'd gotten shit from Dad and shit from us. Ours had been done in the loving, big-brother way, but still. He'd gotten it from both sides. He wasn't coming back here.

Oh, sure, he'd play with all of us, no problem. But I think he liked the freedom he had not being here.

The plane finally landed at the airport, and there was a car that I recognized waiting for us.

Everly was there leaning against her silver Chevy Trax and she was more beautiful than she'd been when I'd left her.

Silas, Brooks, and I each carried our own bags. We had more at the hotel, but the team would make sure that got back to us. And if it didn't, we didn't give a fuck. I walked directly to Everly, dropped my bag, and wrapped my arms around her, leaning some of my weight onto her. Not all of it. That would have been too much.

"I'm so sorry," she whispered low enough that I was probably the only one to hear her.

"Thanks." Then I pulled back and grabbed my bag again. "What are you doing here?" I asked as I led her to the hatch at the back where Silas and Brooks were already loading their bags.

"I talked to Camden. She said she was ordering

you a car and… This was something that I could do. I wanted to do something."

I pulled her into me for a one-armed squeeze. "Give me your keys." It wasn't that she couldn't drive. She'd driven us before. Driving to the hospital was something active that I could do. If she fought it, I wouldn't push, but I needed us to get there before something bad happened. Our last update still didn't give us much information.

Thankfully, she handed the keys over to me without an issue.

"I can sit in the back," she said. "You guys are way taller than me."

"We're fine," Brooks said before hopping into the back seat.

I made sure that Everly was in the passenger seat with her arms and legs inside before I shut her door. Silas slid in behind the driver's seat. When I hit the button to put the seat back—my girl was a lot shorter than me—Silas grunted.

"Fuck," he said. "Are you trying to amputate me back here?"

I chuckled. "Sorry. I need the room I need."

"I said I'd sit back there," Everly protested.

I snorted. "You don't need to."

"Yeah," Silas said through gritted teeth. "I'm dandy back here."

While Silas dealt with whatever was happening to him in the back seat, I got us out of the airport and onto the road.

"Thanks for coming," Brooks said and Silas agreed. "Did Camden tell you anything?"

Everly shook her head. "She said she didn't have much to tell. Oh." She snapped her fingers. "She did say your brother was driving up. They were in Cincinnati, and none of the flights were good enough. According to her, he said that he could get here faster by walking."

I had to laugh along with Silas and Brooks because that sounded just like something Cobb would say. He was such a younger brother.

A short while later, we arrived at the hospital. I'd barely turned her car off when I opened my door to get out. None of us wanted to miss our chance to say goodbye to our grandpa. He'd been the one who would come pick us up to take us for candy even when Dad had said we couldn't have any because it wasn't what ballplayers did. We'd been seven or ten years old at the time.

There were a lot of vacations that Grandpa had gone with us on. Grandma too until she'd died.

This fucking sucked.

As soon as Amity saw us coming down the hall-way, she hurried right into Silas's arms. The rest of us kept walking so they'd have a minute alone.

It was nice to have someone to go through this with, even if I wasn't spilling my emotions to her. Her being here was all I needed.

"Hey, boys." Mom hugged each one of us. She looked tired as hell. Normally, Mom was like a four-year-old on a five-hour-energy-drink high. Right now, she was moving slower. She was wearing jeans and T-shirt, which was rare. Normally, she wore business suits. And her hair was pulled back into a very small ponytail at the base of her neck. Mom didn't look old enough to have all of us but right now, the corners of her eyes sagged with exhaustion and the lines in her forehead deepened with concern.

"We don't know much," she said. "He had a stroke, but until he's on the mend, we won't really know how bad it was." She led us to the chairs so we could sit. Given the layout, the choice was to have Everly sit on the other side or on my lap, so I pulled her down there. Mom noticed right away and raised an eyebrow.

That was right. She hadn't met Everly yet.

"Mom, Everly. Everly, Mom." And that was all the introduction either of them was getting right now.

"Right. Nice to meet you." Mom wet her lips. "They said he's got some weakness on his left side, but they don't know if that's permanent. They don't know if anything's permanent. But right now, they're concerned about his lungs. They're not good on an average day and he aspirated some vomit not long after the stroke, so they've got him on antibiotics and we have to see how it goes."

As if it were my first time thinking about him, I glanced around to find my dad, yet there was no sign of him.

"Mom," I started. "Where's Dad?"

She took a deep breath and sat up straighter. "He went to get me some food. Says I have to eat, but I'm not hungry."

"You have to eat," Brooks agreed.

That was one thing I had to give my father. He seemed to really love my mom. Or at least he took care of her. I guess one doesn't always mean the other.

Mom offered for all of us to go home, but we weren't going anywhere. This was why we'd come, so this was where we'd stay. We'd lost an hour getting back and as it got later, we sent Amity and Everly to get some sleep.

"You're sure you want me to go?" Everly asked. "I don't mind staying."

"I'm sure. It's just a lot of waiting and at some point, they're going to send us home too."

"You'll call if you need me?" She looked up at me with those big, green eyes full of concern.

"Of course I will. Now go." I gave her ass a quick tap so she'd know I meant it.

Everly smiled, but it was small and tired. I could see she didn't want to leave but was doing what I'd asked her to.

In the end, we only stayed another hour before heading out ourselves. Dad had brought a ton of food and jumped every time he thought Mom needed something. She was going to stay and so was he until she left. But there was nothing more we could do tonight and the hospital said no one would be seeing Grandpa tonight other than Mom, who'd just come out of his room.

He was sleeping, she said, and we should try to get rest, too.

I thought about heading to Everly's, but it was late and she had work in the morning. Though I hoped she'd call in, I probably should've asked her to do it but I'd call her in the morning.

Morning came early and I'd gotten shitty sleep, anyway. The thing that woke me up today was the banging on my front door. After glancing at my phone to make sure I hadn't missed anything, I headed for the door, hoping that Everly had read my mind and taken the day off.

Disappointment ran through me when I swung the door open without checking.

Fuck. Me.

It was Analise, the model I'd been seeing right before I'd left Florida. She had a house down there that she spent a lot of time in. But, I hadn't been with her when I'd gotten traded. We'd been in a very casual thing—as in sometimes had sex—a couple of weeks before. She was tall, not much shorter than me, and her legs went on forever.

Even now, standing in front of my door, she was wearing a pair of shorts that were too short and a T-shirt meant to look like she wasn't trying when I knew damn well she'd probably paid five hundred dollars for the thing. She had her light-blonde hair pulled up into a bun and pushed her too-big sunglasses onto her head when I appeared.

"I heard about your grandpa and came right

up." She stepped toward me. "So you have support."

Everyone had heard about Grandpa. Camden had said they'd announced it on TV during the game, so it was no surprise that she'd heard.

"I don't need your support," I told her. "You should leave." We hadn't ever even been together, really. Though she'd been pretty pissed when I'd told her I hadn't wanted to hook up anymore. I probably should've predicted that she'd pop up again one day.

She'd always said we were dating. We weren't. Sometimes we'd been at the same party, we'd fuck, then go our separate ways.

It hadn't been a commitment. Not like I have with Everly and the last thing I wanted was for her to hear about this. I'd tell her before anyone else could.

"Urban…" She dropped her voice. "I know we haven't talked in a couple of weeks so that you could cool down—"

I furrowed my brows in confusion. "Cool down from what? We weren't dating. We didn't break up. We were fucking. Nothing more."

Her head snapped back. "You don't mean that. You're just hurting."

I shook my head. "I'm not."

Analise gave me that sweet smile she used to get whatever she wanted. As if she needed it. She was a fucking model. People fell all over themselves for her.

"Now, Urban." She reached out and touched my chest. I grabbed her wrist to stop her, but at the same time, I heard someone *tsk* in the hall.

My gaze swung over in time to see Everly square her shoulders and shake her head. "Fucking predictable." She dropped the drink holder that had two coffees and tossed a bag at me. Then she turned and stopped down the hall.

She'd brought me breakfast.

And found me with the model.

Normally, I'd say a guy's girl should give him a chance to explain instead of assuming and storming off.

But this was Everly we're talking about. She'd once walked in on the man who'd professed his love to her fucking her damn sister.

This wasn't something she could be rational about in the moment.

I wanted to push past Analise and chase Everly, but I was in my boxer briefs and nothing else. Plus, Analise would follow me and the last thing I wanted to do was put the two of them in the same place at the same time.

Analise could be a bitch and I wouldn't put it past her to make Everly think she'd been leaving my apartment after spending the night when she abso-fucking-lutely hadn't been.

"You're going to wait three minutes, and then you're going to leave." I stepped closer to her. "If that woman you just saw is anywhere you are, you aren't going to speak to her. Do you understand?"

"Urban, you're being ridiculous."

But I slammed my door and turned the lock to ensure she wouldn't try to get inside. If she was still there once I had clothes on to go after the woman I loved, I'd call the police.

I didn't care what happened as long as I could get to Everly before she got lost in her own thoughts.

CHAPTER 19
EVERLY

Seeing that tall, gorgeous woman outside of Urban's apartment—in front of which he was standing there in just his boxer briefs—brought everything from my past speeding forward and had my stomach threatening to revolt.

The joke was on my stomach, given that I had nothing in there to come up if it did.

He'd been touching her. Maybe if he hadn't been touching her, I wouldn't have lost my shit… No. I would have.

Fuck.

I slammed my hand against the steering wheel of my car as I drove away.

No doubt Urban would hurry down after me and try to say that it wasn't what it had looked like.

Wasn't that what cheaters always said? That somehow the one being cheated on had seen it wrong?

What a bunch of bullshit. When I'd just decided to risk my heart… Well, this sealed it up. I wouldn't be doing this again, and I didn't care if that meant I was alone forever. I had Jade.

First, I called the camp to tell them I wasn't feeling well and wouldn't be in today. In the years I'd worked there, I hadn't called in a single time, so they had to take me seriously. Of course they were understanding and told me it wasn't a problem. We always had a plan B and with the team being on a road trip, they could easily change the plan for my campers.

Then I had to decide where to go.

Home was out. Urban could show up there. Instead, I decide to drive to the entire other side of town to a coffee shop that I'd never been in. Wallowing in public would ensure that I wouldn't waste tears on yet another asshole.

My phone buzzed with messages, but I didn't even bother looking. They could've been from Urban or they might not have been. To me, it didn't matter. I was sick today and everyone else could fuck off.

The coffee only lasted so long before I was back in my car deciding what I should do. After checking the time, I realized the morning class Jade had signed up to teach last week was about to start and it would be a perfect place to hide.

Not hide. No. Everly Rose wasn't going to hide from some mediocre man.

But that was the problem, wasn't it? The others had been mediocre, but Urban wasn't.

I pulled my car into a tight space at the gallery where Jade was teaching the course. I still had a few minutes and hoped that they would allow a late registrant. I didn't care about learning to paint, but I wanted to be close to my best friend.

Inside the gallery, I was stopped at the desk because yeah, you had to pay.

"Did you preregister?" the woman asked. Her hair was an unnatural black cut very short into an artsy shape. Jade was artsy, but this woman was *avant-garde*, and it fit her. She was beautiful.

"I did not. I am hoping I still can."

She started shaking her head as soon as I said I hadn't registered. Well, she'd looked nice enough when I'd come in.

"I'm sorry, but the class is full." There was a

hint of an accent to her words. One that I couldn't place.

"Janine," Jade called out as she was gliding toward us. Jade didn't walk when she was in art mode. She glided. "This is my best friend, Everly. We have room for her."

"But there are—"

"We have room," Jade insisted. "Don't worry about the fee. I doubt she'll paint anything."

Janine grunted, but Jade guided me away from her.

"Not everyone is here yet," she whispered. "We have a few minutes." And she didn't stop until we were in the room with four other women sitting behind canvases on easels waiting for the class to start.

Jade sat down on a chair near where her easel was and pulled me into the one next to her.

"What are you doing here?" she asked. "You don't even like art."

"I like art," I challenged. "I like looking at it. It's not my fault if I have no talent."

Jade rolled her eyes. "You have skills you could hone."

I sighed. "I'm here because I've had a shit

morning." My voice came out barely above a whisper.

She moved around her canvas and sat on the other chair next to me. "What happened?" Another woman came in and took a spot. "We're waiting on one more, so what's the condensed version?"

"I saw a woman at Urban's apartment this morning," I said, keeping my voice down low enough so that the other women wouldn't hear me. "I know it's not his sister and he was mostly naked, so…"

She closed her eyes then opened them slowly. "That rat bastard. What'd he say?"

My eyes widened. "I didn't wait around to find out which excuse he was going to use," I told her. "I wanted to keep some dignity here."

Jade reached out and set her hand on mine. "You have to give him a chance to explain."

"Do I?" I took a deep breath. I'd heard the schtick before. "Do I owe him anything?"

"I think you do."

"What?" This came out much louder than I'd intended.

Jade's eyebrows rose then her eyes narrowed as she stood up. "We're waiting on Christine. You can all start painting your background the color of your choice based on my example." There was a second easel that I hadn't noticed with a complete painting sitting on it.

It was like I'd forgotten Jade always did the painting ahead of time so the people who took her class would know how it's supposed to look when she taught them a technique. The painting was beautiful. But then she pulled me out of the room.

"You have to let him explain, Everly. Why would a guy chase after you just to cheat on you as soon as you agree to give him a shot? And why would he have her at his apartment knowing you could show up at any time?"

Valid questions that I hadn't taken the time to consider, but I didn't care.

"I did everything I told myself I wouldn't do. I broke a promise to myself, Jade. A promise that I'd made so that I wasn't the one to get hurt again. What the hell is wrong with me?" I ranted, which prompted her to take me into another room. "Why do these people look at me and say, 'Yup, it'll be fun to crush her spirit'?"

Her face softened. "There's nothing wrong with you, Everly. The past was just immature boys who took advantage when an opportunity presented itself. This isn't that."

"How do you know?"

"I guess I don't. But if you don't at least talk to him, then you not only broke a promise to yourself, but you also broke the rules of conflict resolution. You can't run away from the problem."

I stuck my bottom lip out like a two-year-old. "What if *I'm* the problem?"

She snickered. "You're not."

Shaking my head, I told her, "I can't do it right now. Not today. I'm too…" I shook out my entire body. "I just can't."

She held up her hands in defeat. "Then don't, but know the longer you leave it ,the worse it's going to get."

She wasn't wrong, but right this moment, I was honestly too scared to find out the truth.

Was it logical? Probably not. Were people always logical? No, they weren't and right now, I had to do what was right for me.

But I also couldn't be a whiny, little bitch about it and ignore all phone calls because I didn't want to talk to him.

Sitting in my car outside of the art gallery, I checked my phone. It had been him who'd called three times and there was at least one text message from him as well. I didn't know how many because

I wasn't going to click on it to see. Then he'd know that I'd read it.

Finally, I went home. With the unexpected day off, the apartment needed a good cleaning. I could hide away from the world inside my own home. With earbuds in and music playing loudly, I wouldn't even notice if someone came over.

That night, my phone rang for the first time in hours. I'd just taken a shower and put on my pajamas after working up a good sweat cleaning.

It was Camden, so I answered.

"Are you all right, Everly?" she asked when I answered.

"I'm… fine. Is something wrong?"

There was silence on the other end, but it sounded like distant or muffled voices in the background then she came back. "No. Nothing new, anyway." Then she sighed. "My brother hasn't been able to get a hold of you, so we've been worried."

"I didn't mean to worry you," I told her. "I would've answered if *you* called." But that sounded bitchy to my ears. "I mean, I wasn't ignoring *you*."

"Can I come over?" she asked, which took me by surprise.

Could she? Camden and I had become friends

and we hadn't argued or anything, so there was no reason not to see her.

"Sure. You can come over. Alone."

She snorted. "I wasn't going to invite anyone else."

Twenty minutes later, Camden was at my door with Chinese food.

"You brought food?" I asked as she came in.

"In case I was hungry," she said. "I don't know what you've been doing and besides, food gives you something to do with your hands."

That much was true and I loved food anyway.

"Want to eat at the coffee table in the living room?" I asked her as I went to get plates. "Jade and I do that all the time."

"Sounds good to me."

Once we were set up, I knew I had to apologize to her. We were friends and I hadn't been a good one today.

"I'm sorry, Camden. I should've reached out to you to see how your grandpa's doing."

"Thank you for saying that." She took a bite of noodles. "He's all right for now. More alert today. They don't think he's going to die in the near future but also don't know what that future holds. They said infections are common after this kind of stroke and can be pretty dangerous, especially for him, so we're all wearing masks and gowns to go in and see him."

"That's good." I squeezed her hand. "I'm glad that for now he's out of immediate danger."

"Me too." She sat back with a piece of orange chicken on her fork and held it like a popsicle. "It's weird. He's been here my whole life and has been a big part of it. I just don't think he's been the same since our grandma died."

"How long ago was that?" I slipped a piece of beef in my mouth. It was normal to talk while eating, even if this was a less-than-pleasant topic.

"Five years ago… no, six. They were together forever and it had taken a lot for him to win her over." She shrugged. "They were inseparable. But then she died. He tried to be strong for the rest of us. We could still see how sad he was." She glanced at me then stared blankly at the TV. "That's why we all pretended to do better than we were. So he wouldn't worry."

That information tugged at my heartstrings. I hadn't met everyone in their family, other than briefly at the hospital, though I still hadn't been face to face with their brother Cobb. He hadn't been there yet when I left the hospital. Their dad, I briefly met. And when I say briefly, he said hello and that was it. He'd been busy with their mother.

"It sounds like you grew up in a great, loving family," I told her. What I didn't say was that it sounded leaps and bounds better than what I'd had growing up.

"We did. Mostly. My dad was so damn hard on the boys. He's hard on me, but it's different. I have a vagina, so I was never going to play baseball professionally. Plus, I will argue to the death with him over anything. I challenge him, where the guys tend to avoid the fight and do whatever they want. Unless it's really important." She shifted to the side. "Like my dad and Silas had a blowup over Amity a little while ago. But that was because my dad was being a fucking asshole."

Well, that was confusing. Having met Amity, I couldn't see why anyone would dislike her. "Amity?" I asked. "Why? She's great."

She nodded. "She is. But my dad really wanted the guys to still be in their *fuck 'em and forget 'em* era. Women are a distraction, so…"

"Ah, yes. Baseball is the priority."

"Correct." Then, as if she realized she'd just said something, she snapped up straight. "That's not me saying all of my brothers *are* in their *fuck 'em and forget 'em* era. I wasn't saying that."

Once I was done snickering, I assured her, "I didn't think you were."

She sat back, looking more relaxed. "Good. I said something at our house after the charity game that I think caused a problem between Silas and Amity and I didn't want to be doing that again."

"What'd you say?"

"That I stay away from ballplayers because they're all cheating whores."

Well, didn't that hit the nail on the head? "Right."

"They're not," she said, clearly trying to reassure me. "Silas would cut off his own dick before he'd cheat on Amity. It was just my own shit coming back to haunt me, and Amity grew up around her brother and all of mine. She knew how they'd been back then and… Well, let's just say it didn't go over well with Silas."

"I bet."

She was silent for too long and I knew what was coming next. "Everly—"

"No." I held up my hand like it was a large, red stop sign, telling her to go no further. "I don't want to talk to you about your brother. We're friends and we need to keep that separate if we want to stay friends."

"You're right. I agree. I told him that when he asked me to call you."

Well, fuck. That was something I'd explicitly told him not to do. "Well, that's on him, then. I told him I didn't want him going through you about me. I didn't want us put in that position."

"We won't be again."

"Why did you do it, then? If you agree that our relationship could be kept separate?" I'd wondered that since she'd called.

"He seemed genuinely worried that something might've happened. Seeing how worried he was worried me and I should've called you without telling him that I'd gotten a hold of you, but..." She shrugged. "He was *worried* when he couldn't get a hold of you, Everly."

"Did he tell you what happened?" I asked. She nodded. "Then you know why I'm not going to be answering his calls for a while. I have to be in the right mindset to hear what he has to say and make sure that I'm not going to be a sucker about it."

"I understand."

For the rest of the time that Camden was in my apartment, we didn't mention her brother. That was the best. Whatever happened between Urban and me wasn't going to affect Camden and my friendship.

I was good with that. Urban was still going to text and call, most likely, but I could ignore that. Blocking him crossed my mind but I realized that I wanted to know he was calling.

I just didn't want to answer.

But two days later, the calls and texts stopped and I didn't hear from Urban again.

CHAPTER 20
URBAN

Once we knew that Grandpa wasn't at death's door, Silas, Brooks, and I headed back out to join our team. We only had three days, anyway. It was only two more games on the road, but our first one back, we lost.

It was like everyone on the team hadn't had his head in the game. I sure as fuck didn't, and that had to change. I'd been so worried about Everly when she wasn't answering my calls that I got distracted. One loss, and I knew that I had to put her out of my head.

Which was why I also stopped calling and texting. If she wanted to talk to me, she'd reach out. I'd done all that I could.

Analise showing up when she had had been bad

timing for me. Analise wouldn't have cared. That was why I hadn't been with her. Not really. She was concerned with status, and dating a professional player would've helped that, so we hadn't dated. That didn't mean she hadn't tried to strut me around her friends. The problem was that I didn't strut on command. Any game she and her friends had come to had been her doing, even if she'd told them that I'd made it happen.

Not a chance. I'd had her number early, and while she'd been happy to be the release I needed when I needed it, she wasn't the kind of woman I would've been serious with.

She was too wrapped up in that other world.

In the end, she hadn't been Everly.

I hadn't been looking for Everly when I'd found her, but when I'd met her, I'd known she was what I was looking for. Which was why fucking around wasn't enough for me with her.

Now, through no fault of my own, I'd lost her.

I'd let her down by being in that position. I'd let my team down. I was letting myself down.

It wasn't until we pulled back into Kalamazoo that I had things right in my head again.

The bus got to the field around ten, which was just enough time for us to get ready for our home game tonight. It'd been three days since I'd talked to Everly and for the first time, I'd successfully gotten her mostly out of my head.

We'd gone through our normal routines and were on a break for food, but I was going to eat quickly and use the time for something else.

"I'm going to check on Grandpa," I told Brooks and Silas. "Anyone want to come?"

"Yeah." Brooks threw his shin pad into the locker. "I'll come."

"I'll come too." Silas pulled his shirt off so he could change. We weren't going to the hospital in our warm-up uniforms and he'd already changed.

Luckily for us, the hospital was only a few blocks from the field. Camden was coming out as we were going in.

"I'll catch up," I told my brothers. They kept walking, but I pulled my sister to the side so we'd be out of the way of anyone else in the hospital. "How's he doing?"

She shrugged. "He's all right. I think it's hard for him not to be able to talk clearly, but he seems to be in good spirits."

"He still can't talk?" I asked. She shook her head. "Is that permanent?"

"They don't know. They'll have a better handle on it once he can start therapy."

"Good." That was all I'd wanted to know, but still, I stood there like I was waiting for something else.

"What?" she asked.

"Have you talked to—"

"Nope." She started walking away from me. I had to hurry to catch up to her.

"Camden, what the hell are you doing?"

"Getting away from you."

"Why?" I hadn't even finished my question.

"Because you're going to ask if I've talked to Everly. And I'm going to see concern and hurt in your eyes and want to tell you everything." Finally, she stopped and turned to me. "But I can't. She and I agree that our friendship can't be intertwined with whatever is happening between the two of you. I swear my brothers are trying to keep me from having friends. Next thing I know, one of you is going to fall for Harlowe."

I snorted. "It won't be me." Harlowe was great. But she wasn't who I wanted. I wanted Everly.

"Good to hear. But I have other brothers."

I shrugged. "Only Cobb, who isn't here, and Brooks are even available."

She glanced away from me nervously. "Aren't *you* available?"

Well, fuck. She might as well have punched me in the damn stomach.

Yeah. I was available right now, but I didn't want to be. It was up to Everly if I stayed that way.

"Fine," I told her. "I get what you're saying. I won't ask anything other than if she's OK. Is she OK? I at least need to know that."

Camden wet her bottom lip and looked up at me the way she had when she'd been a kid. "She's managing. She's all right. I don't know if I'd jump to *OK*. But that's all I can tell you."

"Thank you," I said quietly, then I pulled her into my arms for a big hug. Camden really did do the most for this family. She was so on top of everything and wanted to take care of everyone.

She was also the one who would put us in our places at the snap of a finger.

She said it was all about balance.

Once she got on the elevator, I went to my grandpa's room, as I'd intended when I'd gotten here. I couldn't have known that I would run into my sister or that we'd have the talk that we had.

For now, I was putting Everly out of my mind and focusing on the things I could control. Because whether she spoke to me again or not wasn't one of those things.

Camden had been right. Grandpa was frustrated that he couldn't communicate with us the way that he would want to. We got what he was saying, but it was slurred and slow and came with a lot of drool that irritated him.

"At least he's doing better," Silas said as we headed back to the baseball field. Brooks had driven us, so when he pulled the car into a parking spot, we all hopped out.

"Yeah, that's something," Brooks added.

"Do either of you ever think about what it'd be like to have something happen to you?" I asked him and this probably wasn't the time for this conversation.

"Like a stroke?" Silas asked.

"Not necessarily," I told him. "We do have a ball flying at our faces at a hundred miles an hour every day. A bad head injury can fuck you up."

"Yeah." Brooks was the first to admit it. "I've thought about it. But it's risk-reward, right?"

I snorted. "Are you saying that being paid millions of dollars a year is worth the possibility of becoming a vegetable because of an errant fastball?"

He pulled the door to the stadium open. "Is that what we all decided when we chose to do this?"

"He's right," Silas said. "A career-ending injury would fucking suck, but what's the alternative? Working in an office? We love this game. Love playing it. None of us would be happier doing anything else. Now, after our careers are over? Sure. There're tons of things we might do and love, but now? Fuck no."

Yeah. That much was true. If you got hurt in this game, at least you got hurt doing something that you loved.

And right now, I had to get ready to do thing that I loved most in this world. Well… it might've been second- or third-most, but as far as a job went, I couldn't love anything more.

We were out warming up on the field when I saw Camden and Amity come down toward our dugout and take a seat where Dad's season tickets were. I didn't know if they were season tickets. All I knew is that was where the family sat.

It was a rough game. Every time we scored, the other team answered. In the end, we won, but there'd been too many mistakes. Coach was going to tear into us for that.

When I came out of the shower, my brothers

and Jenner were right behind me. The clubhouse was quieter after the game, even when we won. Maybe *quieter* wasn't the right word, but less loud. We were no longer trying to hype each other up for the game and most of us were tired, ready to relax a little before we had to do it all over again.

"How come we haven't seen Everly around?" Brooks asked. I'd been very good at keeping all that shit to myself.

"Yeah. You fuck up already?" Silas added.

I scowled at both of them. "Neither of you know what you're talking about."

"No, seriously," Brooks said after they'd both stopped laughing. "Where's she been? Can't be work. She works at the camp. They're closed at night."

When I didn't answer, Silas said, "Uh-oh. He fucked up bad."

Shaking my head, I turned to him, "Shut the fuck up. I didn't do shit."

Brooks came over closer and leaned against the edge of the cubbies. He wasn't wearing a shirt yet, and a bruise was forming near his shoulder from a hard slide into home in the sixth inning. My brother got beat up at the plate sometimes. "Seriously. What happened? I'm helpful. Ask Silas."

Silas sighed with a hard breath. "I'm not backing that up."

I snorted. Silas had been a fucking idiot with Amity and it had almost cost him her. He was just lucky that the girl had been in love with him since she'd been, like, fourteen. Otherwise, he wouldn't have gotten a second chance. Wait. He was probably luckier that she knew him so well. Silas had carried a lot of guilt for a lot of years and it was nice to see him shed that.

He seemed lighter these days.

"Seriously." Brooks slapped my arm gently.

I rolled my eyes then dropped into my chair. None of us had gotten fully dressed yet, but we did all have pants on. Jenner was there, as always, right on the edge, listening but not interjecting… yet. He was basically one of us and would interject at some point.

"Fine." I sighed. Unloading my woman problems to my brothers in the locker room hadn't really been on my agenda for today, yet they weren't going to let it go, so here we were. "The morning after she was at the hospital, Everly showed up at my apartment with coffee and pastries before she needed to get to work."

"How sweet," Brooks deadpanned because he

knew there was more coming. It *had* been a sweet gesture on Everly's part.

"Yeah, well, she found me standing at my door with my hand around Analise's wrist."

Brooks furrowed. "Analise?"

"That hot-as-fuck model you were with?" Jenner asked. As I'd said, he'd interject eventually.

"Sure," I told him. Back when we'd been casually having sex, I had found Analise 'hot as fuck,' as Jenner had said. She was a beautiful woman, there was no denying that and my lack of interest didn't impact that. But she wasn't for me. She was probably for someone, but it wasn't me. Getting to know what she was really about had killed all of that.

Brooks furrowed his brows and folded his arms over his chest. "What was she doing there, Urban?"

"She heard about Grandpa. Said she wanted to be there for me."

Jenner snorted, then said, "I bet."

"Anyway..." I gave him a pointed look that hopefully told him to shut the fuck up. "She touched my chest, which was bare since I was in my boxers, and I grabbed her wrist to pull her hand away. Everly was in the hallway right after."

"Why were you still touching her?" Brooks had always been a dad-like figure in our lives. He was always trying to get us to see what we'd done wrong. Shit, when we'd been kids, he'd be there doing something stupid with us, then lecture us about why it had been a bad idea.

"I hadn't had a chance to let go," I told him, which was the truth. I'd pulled her hand away and held it for a second so she wouldn't try it again. But even I had to admit that to Everly, it had probably looked bad.

"And why were you in your underwear?" Silas asked, raising his eyebrow.

"Because she woke me up. I thought it would be Everly at the door, so I didn't bother putting pants on." I pushed to my feet. "Listen, I'm not going to talk about this anymore. I understand how bad it looked. That's why I called her and texted like crazy. She didn't answer and Camden won't tell me anything."

Brooks snorted. "You can't go through our sister just because she's friends with your girl."

"I really hope that bites you in the ass one day," I told him without malice. He couldn't understand because he'd never been in my position.

It fucking sucked. While I'd known I wasn't supposed to go to my sister, knowing hadn't stopped me because I'd been desperate.

"Anyway…" I pushed to my feet and grabbed a shirt then pulled it over me and shoved my feet into my shoes. After grabbing my bag, I said, "You can all fuck off." Then I left the clubhouse to the roar of their laughter.

Assholes.

I grabbed dinner then went home and turned on the sports channel to see what they were saying about our game. It wasn't great, but neither had been the game. They rode the pitcher hard because he'd given up so many runs that I couldn't believe the coach hadn't taken him out sooner. Though given a couple of injuries, I could see why he needed the pitchers to last as long as they could.

My dinner was half gone when my phone vibrated with a text message. At first, I was going to ignore it on the chance that it was one of my asshole brothers. But Grandpa was still in the hospital, so ignoring anything wasn't a real option. If something happened with him, I'd want to know, but I sure as hell hoped no one would send me bad news with a text.

It wasn't about my grandpa.

It was Everly.

I'm sorry I didn't answer your calls and messages. Please call me when you have time to talk.

I sat back and sighed.

Did I want to talk to her? Fuck yes.

Did I think it'd go the way that I wanted? That, I figured, was probably a no.

I'd promised Everly that I wouldn't tell her how I felt unless she told me first. A stupid fucking promise I'd made just so that she wouldn't freak out and bolt. But a promise I'd intended to keep. If I talked to her now, I wasn't so sure that I could and given how late it was and my schedule tomorrow, I didn't think it the best idea to start a whole thing tonight.

Tomorrow would be better.

But I wasn't so sure the conversation would be worth it. Everly absolutely was, but I didn't have the best feeling that a conversation would go my way, that she'd let me explain, that her hurtful past wouldn't keep her from being with me. If I had to deal with all of that, I wanted to do it when I wasn't so exhausted.

Again… tomorrow would be better.

CHAPTER 21
EVERLY

O.K.

That was all I got? I'd told him I wanted to talk to him and all I'd gotten was 'OK'?

Had I expected that Urban Briggs would fall all over himself to get to me the minute I got my head out of my own ass? Well, no. I hadn't. But I'd thought he'd at least say he wanted to talk to me or see me. Something.

Instead, I'd gotten 'OK.'

Sure, it'd taken too many days to pull my head from my ass. Or, in other words, allow Jade to get through to me. Sometimes, I wondered why she was my friend. Not really, but every once in a while… I was a lot to deal with. The family shit she'd been through with me over the years. The heartbreaks she'd nursed me through. Now me getting in my own way when there was a man who might actually be good for me.

That wasn't to say that I hadn't been there for her. I'd shown up to her house the two times she'd had her heart broken. We'd talked through the night and eaten ice cream and made lists on why she was too good for whoever had broken up with her.

It was give and take. That was how best friends worked.

Now… it might all be too late.

"Well?" Jade asked me the next morning at camp. Baseball camp was over for a few weeks and a new group of kids would be starting the next session. That meant no players today and it wouldn't have been Urban's day anyway.

There was no way I'd see him today unless I made it happen.

"He said 'OK.' That's it."

She was standing outside of the art room in a camp T-shirt, white shorts, and Converse tennis shoes, looking like the epitome of summer. Her hair was pulled into a bun with little strands having fallen out.

Jade was the only person I knew who'd wear white shorts to do art. But she wouldn't care if she got paint on them. It was just the way she was. Any sacrifice for the art.

"That's it?" She put her hands on her hips, like she was about to give someone the business. It wasn't me, so it had to be Urban.

"Yeah." I shrugged. "Listen. It's my fault. We established that. I should've given him a chance to explain. He doesn't owe me anything. I made assumptions and let the walls I've carefully built up stop me from hearing him out." I looked her in the eye. "It's my fault. If he doesn't want to talk to me, it's my fault."

I walked over to the cooler that was sitting nearby waiting for water to be loaded into it. I was taking the kids to the water this morning because it was so warm, they were going to need two cool offs. First, we were going to hike through the woods and talk about the science of nature. Science wasn't my thing, but I enjoyed nature. Good thing I wouldn't be leading this and was there as an extra counselor.

"That's such bullshit," she spat like she was seriously angry. "Yes, you did do all those things, but I think that man loves you, so he should—"

"Whoa." I stopped right in front of her. "Don't

go talk about that love stuff. No one said anything about love."

Pursing her lips, she cocked her head to the side. "Everly, Urban can't tell you he loves you. He promised not to say anything that would freak you out until you said it first."

Well, damn. She was right. Good thing I'd told her everything. I'd forgotten that promise in the mess of my own thoughts and emotions.

Did he love me? Could he love me?

I'd been denying all of my feelings for so long that I wasn't sure I could recognize feelings in anyone else anymore. I couldn't trust what I thought I saw.

"I have an idea," I told her. "There's a game tonight. We should go. Maybe I can catch him after. If he doesn't want to see me anymore, that's fine. I fucked up, but at least this way, I'll know."

"I love this. I'll get us tickets."

I'd let Jade get the tickets rather than ask Camden. I might've trusted Camden not to tell her brother things now but I wasn't one hundred percent sure yet. And this was something I thought she might not be able to keep from him.

"I should do that," I countered. "I'm going to

need to be down by the field. Those are probably sold out, so I'll have to go a resale site and they'll probably be expensive."

"Pft." She brushed me off with her fingers then turned me back toward the cooler. "You're going to be in the woods all day. I'll take care of it. You know I don't care about the money."

Because it was easy not to worry about what you were spending when you had money.

"Fine," I agreed because she was right. I couldn't buy tickets from the middle of the woods. We barely got cell reception out there and mostly used walkie-talkies.

"Go. I'll take care of it."

After waving my *thank you* at her, I grabbed the cooler and went to the ice machine to load the thing up. Water was right next the machine, so I got it ready just in time for the campers to show up.

Even with the heat, it was a beautiful day in nature. The kids loved the lessons on everything from moss to the animals they might see. Thankfully, we didn't see some of the scarier specimens, but the black squirrels excited the kids. It wasn't often that they got to see them since we lived in a city.

Then we spent an hour at the water before lunch and filled the afternoon with so much fun that when we went back to the pond, they were all almost too tired to swim. They did float around and splash, though.

I got drenched by some of that splashing, but it had felt good and I wasn't mad at all.

Even driving home wet didn't bother me.

Jade had insisted on picking me up for the game. As she'd put it, if things went right, Urban would be taking me home and she didn't want me to have to worry about my own car. That was fine by me, but I had serious doubts any of that would be happening.

"This place is huge," Jade said when the field first came into view. "This many people like baseball?"

I snorted. "Apparently." She wasn't into sports, either, and it was her first game.

"I wouldn't have imagined," she said. I turned us the right toward where our seats would be. "I mean, it always looks like a lot of people on TV, but… Wait, how many people does this hold?"

I had to think about that, but finally, I came up with the answer. "The last game I was at said it was a sold-out crowd of, like, forty-one thousand."

Her feet stopped and so did she. "Forty-one thousand? Holy shit."

I snickered. "I know. It can be overwhelming. Our seats are this way." I turned and started walking again with the hope that we'd get to our seats while the team was still warming up.

"Look at you knowing your way around."

I shook my head. "I know the general direction our seats are. I wouldn't exactly call that knowing my way around."

"We'll disagree, then."

After work, I'd gone home and showered. Since I was going to a baseball game in this heat, I'd put on distressed jean shorts, a T-shirt, and Converses. Jade was dressed basically the same. Though she had her blonde hair down, I'd pulled mine back into a wavy ponytail.

"Before we go down there, I have to stop at this stand." I pointed to the one nearest us selling T-shirts.

"Yes, right. All part of the plan."

She waited while I bought the Knights T-shirt with Urbans' number on it then hurried into the nearest restroom to change into it. Then I put the old T-shirt into the bag they'd given me. Due to rules at the stadium, I had my phone in one pocket and a small wallet in the other. Bags from the outside weren't allowed.

"Ready?" she asked. I nodded because my nerves were too on edge to speak.

This was an unusual move for me. I hadn't tried with a man for years and now… I was going to go all in, not knowing if he even wanted me to.

If I didn't, I'd regret it the rest of my life.

Did the scene at his apartment look bad? Yeah, it did. But I should've let him explain and trust that he wouldn't lie to me. Trust was such a hard thing for me and me not knowing how to do it might've cost me a man that I… had feelings for.

So what explained the woman in the hallway? I didn't know and really didn't love any of the scenarios that I'd come up with. I had to hope it was a fan that showed up at his apartment or something similar. Anything but what I worried about.

Jade had done an excellent job of picking tickets. We were right down by the Knights' dugout. My timing was right. The guys were still out on the field, stretching and warming up. When they started jogging toward the dugout, I twisted my fingers together.

"Don't worry," Jade said while patting my hands. "It'll be all right."

Would it?

I didn't know.

Then I saw him and my heart beat wildly out of control, forcing my breaths to come faster. Seeing Urban shouldn't have made me nervous, but given the fact that he could react in a very bad way, it did.

As he got to the steps of the dugout, he slowed to a walk. He scanned across the stands near him, flying over me as if he didn't even see faces. Then he stopped and his gaze came right back to me.

He paused quickly and all I could do was stare. Then I raised my hand in front of my chest to wave, but he didn't wave back. Instead, his jaw tightened before he went into the dugout.

"He hates me," I said quietly.

"No," she said, but she chuckled and I couldn't see what would be so funny. "He definitely doesn't. He's surprised you're here, but he knows he needs to focus on the game."

And that was the explanation I was going to go with.

"Hey," Camden said suddenly right beside me as she dropped into the empty seat there. I'd hoped no one was going to sit there in case I needed a quick getaway, but if someone was, then I was glad it was her. "I didn't know you two were coming. I could've gotten you seats. I'm Camden," she said to Jade.

That was right. They hadn't met yet. "Sorry," I told her. "This is my best friend, Jade. Jade, Camden."

"What's it like having such hot brothers?" Jade asked after the niceties were out of the way.

Rolling her eyes, Camden said, "Awful. I've had people try to use me to get to them and it doesn't help that my brothers know they're hot commodities. Cocky, little bastards."

The three of us giggled.

"But I'm glad I met you, Jade," Camden said. "We could form a little girl gang of our own."

I groaned. "I'm not up for getting jumped."

She snorted. "Me, either. I just meant, you, me, Jade, Amity, and Harlowe. We'd almost have the guys outnumbered."

I furrowed my brows. "Listen, I'm an English teacher, so math isn't my thing, but you only have four brothers and there'd be five of us."

"Right." She snapped her fingers. "But we have to include Jenner. He's an honorary Briggs and unfortunately, nothing I've done has scared him away yet."

Jenner. Yes. Of course. I hadn't talked to him

too much, but he did seem to be part of the family, from what I'd heard.

The three of us chatted as we watched the game. I was surprised by how much I'd picked up in the few short weeks I'd been with Urban.

Been with. I shook my head at myself. Even I couldn't deny that we'd been together.

I'd been so stupid about this. No. I hadn't been stupid. I'd been blinded and obsessed with protecting my heart.

Not anymore. Sure, Urban may break it today, but he was worth the risk.

"I have a question," I asked her after the seventh-inning stretch. "I know I shouldn't ask you, but I don't have anyone else to ask."

"Shoot."

"Is there any chance of me getting a pass to go down to the clubhouse to talk to Urban?"

She raised an eyebrow. "You want to talk to my brother?"

Nodding, I told her, "I want to apologize. I shouldn't have run off the way I did and—"

"You ran off?" she asked, clearly having no idea what I was talking about. I hadn't gone into details with her about what had led to me going no-contact with Urban, and I guessed he hadn't, either.

"Yeah. I can explain to you after the game if you want, but I did and it wasn't fair. I should've let him explain. It was because of things other people did in the past. I'd like to apologize."

She smiled widely. "I'll take you down there myself."

Once the game had ended with a win for the Knights, Camden pulled me up without giving me a chance to worry about whether Urban was going to acknowledge me or not. The three of us battled the crowd until we were on the concourse.

"This is where I leave you," Jade said before hugging me. "It's going to be fine. You'll see."

I was glad that she had all the faith in the world. All the faith that I didn't have.

"I don't have my car here," I said suddenly but Camden and Jade looked at me with wide eyes like I'd just grown a second head. "If this doesn't go well. How will I get home." There were several ways for me to get back from the ball park. This wasn't something I should've been concerned about but here we were.

Camden put a hand on each shoulder and told me, "My brother wouldn't leave you stranded no matter what. I can hang around the stadium, though, in case you need a ride."

That would be asking too much so I took a breath. "No. You can go after we get down there. I was being dumb. I can get a ride share or a bus if I have to."

With that settled, Jade headed for her car and Camden started me toward the clubhouse.

As we walked, I told her what had happened between Urban and me. She listened patiently without interrupting me even as I tried to justify everything I'd done.

I wouldn't do that with Urban.

"I assumed you would've heard," I told her after we'd gotten through the first door.

"No. My brothers don't tell me stuff like that most of the time."

"Well, that's it. That's what I did. Kept him at arm's length for too long then as soon as I let him close, I found a way to fuck it up."

She shrugged. "I probably would've done the same thing. That's why I won't date a pro athlete. I don't think I could stand seeing someone else touching him, even if he was putting a stop to it." Then she sighed. "Well, that's one of the reasons."

Finally, we were in the spot we normally waited for the guys. It was away from the clubhouse doors so we couldn't be a distraction but in the perfect spot to be the first thing they'd see when they came out.

"My brother might have tried to tell me," she confessed. "At the hospital. He brought you up, but I shut him down because I didn't want whatever happened to interfere with our friendship."

"You were right to do that," I told her. "I asked him not to go through you for things about me for that very reason."

She gave me a smile and squeezed my hand, though I wasn't sure what she was grateful for. It had been decided long ago that the two relationships had to be separate. By me. It was the only way we could ensure that Camden and I could stay friends.

It wasn't too much longer before some of the guys started coming out of the clubhouse. Not the guys we were waiting for… or not *the* guy.

Then finally, Urban pushed through the door. When he saw us he came over and stopped. His gaze slid down my body, leaving a rush of goosebumps to run over my skin. His gaze was like a touch. One I craved.

But he didn't say anything. Then Silas, Brooks, and Jenner came out and saw Urban and I locked in a stare-down.

Brooks wrapped an arm around Camden's neck and pulled her with him. "Let's go, baby sister." Camden groaned but went with him, leaving Urban and me alone.

Well… almost alone.

Bryson came out of the clubhouse next and saw us standing there. He chuckled loudly then kept walking. Good idea on his part.

"He leaving you alone?" Urban asked. A flood of relief washed over me. At least he'd spoken to me. If nothing else, there was that.

"Yes. I haven't heard from him since the last time I told you I had."

"Good." He ran a tongue over his bottom lip. "What're you doing here?"

This was it. This was the moment. It was time for me to come clean and apologize. I just needed him to listen to me.

"I'm here in the hopes that you'll let me explain what happened. I want to apologize and hope you'll forgive me for freezing you out that day. Will you?" I asked. "Will you at least hear me out?"

I'd never been so nervous in my life.

My hands were shaking, and I locked my knees in place to keep me upright. I also bit into my bottom lip to keep from laughing like a deranged hyena—a serious possibility. My heart threatened to escape as it banged harder than ever against my chest.

I promised myself I wouldn't cry if he said *no*.

The problem was, he wasn't saying anything.

CHAPTER 22
EVERLY

"So will you?" I asked after I'd become uncomfortable with the silence.

Urban sighed and nodded. "Yeah. Sure. Not here, though."

I swallowed hard and wrung my hands together. At least he was willing to hear me out. That was something. "OK. Where do you want to go?" I'd have to call for a ride, but I'd meet him anywhere.

"My place?" he asked.

Relief washed over me once again. He didn't want to do this in public. That could've been a good sign or a bad, but I took it as a good one.

"I'll be there."

When I turned to walk back out the way I'd come, Urban grabbed my arm to stop me. "You were with your friend and Camden. Do you have your car?"

"No, but I know how to call a ride share."

He furrowed his brows. "Are you fucking kidding me? You think I'm going to have you call a car when I can just drive you?" His jaw tensed and he shook his head before sighing. "Come on."

The thing was, I *hadn't* thought he'd let me take a car if he'd known I hadn't had one. That wasn't Urban. I just hadn't wanted to assume. He was really upset with me. I'd likely fucked this whole thing up and would have to do some apologizing and explaining. I didn't know if that meant he'd want to be cooped up in a car with me right now.

We were silent on the drive to his apartment. Given that it'd only been days since I'd last seen him, the fact that I felt like it'd been months said something that I could no longer ignore. It wasn't until we were inside his apartment with our shoes off and him heading the kitchen that he said, "Go ahead."

"What?" I'd been too distracted by the way his shirt hugged his broad muscles. Shoulders that I'd hung on to more than once. He was strong everywhere. Probably a byproduct of playing a sport professionally. Whatever it was... I loved it.

"Go ahead," he said again as he pulled the fridge open. "I'm going to make a sandwich. Do you want one?"

I furrowed my brows in confusion. He was going to eat while I poured my heart out to him? Then I realized, this might have been his way of protecting himself too. After all, I'd been the asshole here.

"No thank you," I told him then took a deep breath. "I'm sorry I ran away that day in your hallway." He put his hands on the counter and looked up at me. "That wasn't fair. But I saw… what I saw and something inside me clicked. I had to get away as fast as I could."

"You could've asked what the hell was going on. I would've told you."

All of a sudden, to me, there was too much space between us, so I stepped to the side of the island where he was making the sandwich. Though almost everything was on the counter not being touched. At least I was close enough to touch him if I wanted to.

"I know you would have, but at the time, I couldn't trust myself to tell whether or not what you said was the truth."

"I've never lied to you," he snapped, causing me to close my eyes then open them again.

"I know," I whispered, then I cleared my throat. "But others have and that scared the hell out of me. You were standing there almost naked with a beautiful woman…" I shook my head. The memory of that was worse than the memory of anything else I'd been through. That was how I'd known how I felt about him.

Urban moved a came closer to me, putting a hand on the counter on each side of me and leaned down so that we were eye to eye. "Do you want to know why I was almost naked in my hallway?" No, but I nodded my head slowly anyway. "Because when I heard the knock on the door, I thought it'd be you, so I didn't bother getting dressed thinking that I might just have to get undressed again." He stood up taller and stepped back to lean a hip on the countertop. "That woman was someone I used to see. Not a girlfriend or any of that shit, no matter what she thought. We'd fuck." I winced but hoped that I hadn't shown it. "She heard about my grandpa and came here. Uninvited."

"So you were telling her to leave." I finished the thought for him because now it was clear that was what he'd been doing. Once I allowed myself to think about it, he hadn't looked happy to be standing there. His grip on her wrist was strong but he hadn't been holding onto her as if she was someone special.

If I would've looked longer, I was sure I would've seen more clues.

"Yeah. She touched me, so I grabbed her hand to move it away. You showed up." He wet his lips then went back to pretending to make a sandwich by pulling bread out of the package. "I didn't want her touching me. And don't think I didn't see you flinch when I admitted I'd had sex with her before I met you. We both have pasts. I have to do my job with part of yours."

Yeah. That was right. He had to work with a guy I'd hooked up with, so I could deal with seeing him with one of his, especially since he hadn't wanted her there.

"I'm sorry, Urban. This is all on me, I know that. If this is fucked up with no hope of being fixed, that's on me." I swallowed hard before I said words that I swore I'd never say again. "I fell in love with you probably after the first week but was so afraid that I let this get out of control. I'm so sorry. I'll never ignore your calls again."

Slowly, he set the butter knife down on the

counter and turned to look at me, his hands still on the counter. "What'd you say?"

"That I'm sorry. If you forgive me, I won't ignore your calls again. Hell, I won't ignore them even if you *don't* forgive me."

One corner of his mouth turned up. "You know damn well that's not what I'm talking about."

At first… I didn't know. Then I did. "Oh, that I fell for you after the first week?"

He moved toward me, grabbing my hips when he got close enough and walking me back until I hit the cabinet behind me. "Say it, Everly." The demand in his voice made me catch my breath and caused an aching that only he could relieve. "Say it. Because I promised you I wouldn't until you did."

I bit into my bottom lip with my heart racing and my breath coming quickly. "I love you, Urban Briggs."

I'd barely gotten his name out before his lips crashed into mine. I wrapped my arms around his strong shoulders so that I could lift myself a little more. Urban's hands slid down my body until he cupped my ass and I moaned into his mouth.

It'd only been days since he'd last touched me and I'd missed it as much as I would've missed air.

The intensity between us was something that I'd ignored until now.

I pulled at his shirt so he'd yank it over his head and I could run my nails lightly down his chest. There wouldn't be marks, but I'd know that I'd done it. Made sure that he knew he was mine and I'd be his.

Urban cupped my cheeks as his tongue slid into my mouth, stroking against mine. He walked us to his bedroom, where he gently pushed me back onto the bed. I missed having the contact with him, but when he jerked my shorts and panties down my legs, I realized it had been for a good cause. He shed his pants and boxers quickly then flipped me over.

"You're wearing my name and number on your back." He ran his hands up the backs of my legs and dug his fingers into my ass cheeks.

"I bought it at the game today."

"You should wear something with my name and number on you to every game." He pushed my shirt up, trailing kisses up my spine.

I dropped my forehead into the mattress and allowed the warmth to spread across me. Him. He was the warmth as he hovered over me, his hard cock bouncing against my ass.

"You like that?" I asked once I remembered he'd said I should wear the shirt to his games.

"It's sexy as hell."

I turned so that I could look at him over my shoulder. "Lots of women wear your name and number on their back."

His hand fisted in my hair. "I don't care about lots of women." He moved closer and whispered in my ear, "I love you. Not them."

Closing my eyes, I hoped no tears of relief would fall. It'd send the wrong message but I was so overcome by all things Urban that I couldn't be sure it wouldn't happen. If he was telling me he loved me, then he had definitely forgiven me and that was all I wanted.

Well… maybe not all I wanted.

Urban flipped me onto my back then hovered over me briefly before leaning down to kiss me again. His mouth was warm and his kisses almost brutal, yet I would've taken so much more. The only spot where we were touching was our lips and that just wasn't acceptable.

I slid my hand over each side of his jaw then down his neck to his shoulders. He moved so that he could put all of his weight on one arm. My nails dug into his shoulders when his other hand slid between my legs. He stroked me once gently. Then he worked a finger inside of me.

My head fell back and I groaned.

"All those noises you make are so fucking sexy." His lips met mine again. "You're so fucking sexy."

I didn't need the words, but they didn't hurt.

Urban continued pushing and pulling his finger in and out of me, adding a second and pressing his thumb to my clit. That was all it took. My orgasm hit me as if I'd never had one before, crashing down over me in waves of more pleasure than I'd ever felt before.

"Move up," he told me, so I scurried to the middle of the bed, where my head could rest on the pillows, and watched as he slid a condom down his erection.

Then he was back above me, pushing into me.

Our hands reached everywhere that they could, we kissed and when we needed breath, he'd kiss down my neck, suck softly, or scrape his teeth against my skin. I trailed my nails down his back, making him shudder.

When he stopped, he pressed his damp forehead to mine.

"We need to clean up," he said, sounding as breathless as I felt.

Pushing myself further into the bed, I said, "I don't think I can move."

Urban chuckled then climbed off me, but he pulled me along with him. "You can."

Soon after, we were in the enormous bathtub in his apartment. He was sitting with me between his legs, my back to his chest, trailing the hot water over my skin. He'd asked how hot I liked it, and I told him as hot as he could stand. I was more relaxed with him in that bathtub than I had been anywhere else recently.

"My sister said she'd start looking for a place for me." His chin brushed against the side of my head as he spoke. "You should help her. If you have time."

I leaned back to look up at him. "You want me to help your sister pick out where you're going to live?"

He chuckled. "I'll decide which one. She's going to narrow it down. I don't have the time. But I want you to like whatever I get."

He wanted me to like where he lived. I dropped a kiss to the corner of his jaw then snuggled back down in his arms. "I'll help her. My camp schedule is changing to two days a week. I'll have the time."

"Why is it changing?"

I shrugged. "It's just the camp schedule. Happens every year. Normally, I get another job to fill in the days until they need me five days again."

"Don't," he said, then he squeezed me harder.

I snickered. "I have to. I have bills to pay." Then I sighed. "I'm uncomfortable not making as much money as I can be." Memories began flooding through me but I shook my head and shrugged. "It's a left over thing from my childhood. I know it doesn't make sense. I make decent money. I just feel like something's going to happen and I'll need more then I'll kick myself for not working as much as I can."

Urban nudged me so that I'd move away from him, then he turned me toward him. Knowing that he wanted me close, I climbed onto his lap, straddling him, and placed my hands on his shoulders. His cock hardened beneath me to half capacity. "Don't." He said again, then he nipped at my lips.

Technically, I could choose not to have the summer job. My family's money problems were why I thought I needed to be working every minute. But I had savings and I set up my teacher pay so that I was still getting paychecks in the summer. I'd just have to convince myself that I'd be OK when logic said I would. It was a fear, possibly irrational, but a fear none the less.

There was only one question.

"Why don't you want me to?" I brushed his hair back near his ears.

"It's selfish." He wet his bottom lip. "If you're not working full-time, we'd be able to be together more often. Maybe you could come on a road trip. Even if we can't stay together on the road, we could still spend time together."

Now *that* was an interesting thought. Camden had tried to convince me to come on more than one road trip.

"OK." I shrugged as if it wasn't a big deal but inside I was freaking out. "I won't take on another job."

His hands cupped my ass and squeezed when his mouth met mine. Once he brought the kiss to an end, he said, "I wasn't sure if I should tell you this. Didn't want to freak you out." He ran his fingers down my hair until they met the ends which were wet from the water. "I'm having Camden look for a house instead of an apartment."

I cocked my head to the side. "Wouldn't that be a pain when you leave at the end of the season?" An idea that burned a fiery hole in the pit of my stomach. We'd figure it out, I told myself but it was just another anxiety that I'd have to work through.

As his hands trailed up my back and his arms pulled me closer. "I'm not going anywhere at the end of the season."

My eyes widened. That was something I knew he didn't want to do. "You don't have to stay here for me, Urban. We'll figure it out." Though me moving would mean I'd have to get relicensed in whatever state he ended up in. If he wanted me to come with him at all. We'd stay together no matter what, but he might prefer to focus on the game during the season and just have visits with me. I didn't know.

"Baby, this isn't a hardship. You're here." His hand held the base of my head. "My mom's going to throw a shit ton of money at me to stay. There's no losing with this."

"Only if you're sure."

"Never been more sure about anything."

Soon, all the conversation about houses and being traded and all of that was forgotten so that we could get lost in each other again.

With Urban, getting lost was my favorite thing. I hoped no one would ever find us.

CHAPTER 23
URBAN

Since Everly had come to my apartment and told me she loved me, we hadn't spent a night apart. After this week, her schedule changed, and I hoped she'd be at every game, too. Realistically, that might not have been possible and I was fine with it. But I fucking loved to see her smiling face in the stands.

When I'd told Mom that I'd stay in Kalamazoo for the right price at the end of the season and she should start opening up her wallet, she'd insisted on meeting Everly officially. That quick nothing at the hospital hadn't been good enough. It was like she knew that Everly was the reason I wanted to stay. I did want to stay for her but she was only part of the reason. Being here made me realize that I had a unique opportunity to play with my brothers. I probably shouldn't let that pass by because it wasn't going to last forever.

Grandpa was doing better. Or as better as he could have been. He was in a rehab facility trying to get stronger. Everly and I visited him that Friday and he fucking hated that place. Loved Everly. Grandpa gave me a thumbs-up when I was leaving.

But now, it was Sunday. We'd played a day game and won. Next up, dinner with my family.

Everly had put on a strapless summer dress that and hung to her mid-thigh. It was all I could do not to pull over and yank that top down while pushing her onto my cock. The woman made me feral.

The rest of my family was already at my parents' house when we arrived. I'd told Everly to pack a bathing suit because we'd likely end up in the pool. We normally did. And actually, Cobb was still missing, so I guessed not all of my family was there.

Actually, I hadn't talked to Cobb in a couple of weeks, now that I thought about it.

"This is where you grew up?" Everly asked as I pulled her through the house. It was a summer night. We'd definitely be eating outside.

"Yup."

"This place is insane." The sound of awe in her voice was something I was used to. Most people were in awe of this house. It wasn't my taste but it was a beautiful place to grow up. Especially the back yard. I was huge and almost looked like some tropical paradise in the summer.

I stopped right before going through the French doors that would lead outside. "In more ways than one," I told her, but I wasn't going to elaborate. Not tonight. She'd learn how crazy my family was all in good time.

"You're here!" Mom was the first person we came to. She had been standing near the grill where their personal chef was preparing barbeque chicken and steak. Mom hugged me then stepped back. "Everly, it's so nice to see you again. And this time, under better circumstances."

"It's nice to see you, too, Mrs. Briggs."

"Call me AnnMarie," Mom said, then she pulled Everly over to meet Dad.

I stood tall behind Everly with my hand on her shoulder, ready to yank her out of the way if Dad said anything out of line.

"Conrad, this is Everly." Mom did the introduction, which I thought was for the best. Dad didn't push her the way he pushed the rest of us. And hell, he probably wouldn't even remember seeing her at the hospital.

After greeting her, Dad said, "Is she why you'll stay?"

"Most of the reason, yeah."

His dark eyes leveled on mine as we stood there in a mini stare-down. Then he nodded once and walked away.

"Well, he's learning," Mom told me. "What can I say?"

That had gone better than expected, but it was going to take time to repair my relationship with him. If he even wanted that and it was possible.

Once *meeting the parents* was done with, Everly and I headed over to where my brothers and the other women were sitting and talking. We took a seat at the long table.

"Anyone talk to Cobb recently?" I asked over their chatter.

Brooks furrowed his brows. "No, actually."

"He didn't play on his last start," Jenner told us.

"*What?*" I asked.

Everly leaned into me and whispered, "What does that mean?"

"He's a pitcher, so he starts every five games. He

didn't start in the last game that he was supposed to."

She furrowed her brows. "Is that weird?"

"Yeah." I ran my hand down her back. "It's really fucking weird."

"Mom," Brooks called out, which made her come over. "Have you talked to Cobb? None of us have in a while. I checked my phone and I've called. He just hasn't answered."

"I have." She had that look that told all of us there was something she wasn't saying. "He's all right. No need to worry." Yet everything about her said there *was* a reason to worry.

"Was he hurt?" I asked because that happened in baseball, though I was almost sure I would've seen it on one of the sports shows. We'd all always watched as many of each other's games as we could but with our schedules, it was difficult.

"No." Yet she was being secretive. We all gave her a hard look until she sighed. "He's having a little problem. No need to worry. We'll talk about this later."

Later.

That wasn't the normal way our family handled things. It couldn't have been because Everly and Amity were there because Mom would know anything she told us would go back to them, anyway. Silas and Amity were end game and if I had my way, Everly and I would be too.

It was more likely that she just wanted to get through this dinner without having to deal with it.

The group of us dove into dinner, which was delicious as always, and then dove into the pool. That whole *wait thirty minutes after eating* thing was an old wives' tale, I said. Plus, we weren't exactly breaking Olympic records here.

Watching Everly have a good time with my family made me even more sure about her.

I pulled her over to the side and wrapped my arms around her waist. "I love you, Everly Rose."

A great smile spread across her face. "That's a good thing," she said. "Because I love you more than I should."

Bullshit. She should've loved me as much as she could. There was no too much when it came to us.

Because I didn't think I could love her any more than I already did.

BONUS SCENE

Dear Reader,

I hope you enjoyed Wanting the Player. Urban & Everly were so much fun for me and had me swooning. Urban helping Everly realize that someone can love her without hurting her… chef's kiss. I'm excited for you to see their next step.

I have a bonus scene for you as a thank you for reading. Just click the link below, sign up for my newsletter, and you'll get an email with the bonus scene.

SIGN UP HERE:

https://geni.us/Wanting-Bonus

Meeting a hot baseball player at the courthouse wasn't on my bingo card.

Grabbing coffee after I was arrested—again—is a last minute decision. I know what I'm in for when I get home. Especially since this time, it's for something more than protesting. I've got more trouble than I know what to do with.

Now I'm going to find out what happens when you fall for someone who can't be with you. Trouble just keeps coming.

Winning the Player

He was my brother's best friend and off limits.

The world knows Silas Briggs as the baseball heartthrob on a hot streak. I know him as brother's former friend and my teenage crush.
Four years ago, he broke my young heart by making me think there could be something between us.

Then he left town and never looked back.

Now I'm back and working for the team, hoping that we can be friendly. Then I see him in person and friendship is the last thing on my mind.

START READING KISSING THE PLAYER TODAY

Do you love rock stars?

FOREVER GRAYSON

Forever 18 Book 1

One night three years ago is coming back to haunt me.

It was supposed to be one night then I'd never see him again. One night at a dive bar where I met someone who could scratch an itch.

He wasn't famous then.

Now he's a rock star.

A rock star whose manager just hired me to be the band's stylist. It's a dream job to me but it could be a nightmare.
Is it worse if he remembers me? Or worse if he doesn't?

START READING FOREVER GRAYSON NOW

Cross *Courting Chaos Book 1*

When a sexy drummer mistakes me for a groupie and tries to kick me out of the venue, I'm willing to chalk it up to mistaken identity. Usually everyone knows me but I shouldn't assume. Now Cross wants to make it right ini the hope that my father won't kick his band off the tour.

In trying to make amends, Cross becomes my surprise protector when I accidentally snap some pictures of his bandmate in a bad situation and he wants them deleted.

Cross being my protector has me wanting something I've never wanted before… A sexy drummer.

Growing up with a famous father has taught me many things but the number one rule has always been NEVER FALL FOR A ROCK STAR.

I guess I want to break the rules.

START READING CROSS TODAY

After living under my father's rule, I'm about to break free.

My father has kept me on a short leash my entire life.

The Orin comes for me.

Finding out what he is… scares the hell out of me.

Finding out I'm his supposed mate… I don't know that I'll recover.

START READING MOONSTRUCK TODAY

Being the daughter of my people's leaders, I should understand protocol and appropriate behavior. Problem is, I understand both, I just don't follow them.

But I have a different plan.

There's a boy… now a man, who is supposed to be powerful. I want him on our side.

What I didn't know is that together, he and I might be unstoppable.

Now I just have to find him.

START READING THE GREMLIN PRINCE TODAY

I'm a witch. Or so they tell me.

Finding out I'm a witch isn't even the weirdest part of my day. Having the guy who hated me in high school stand before me to tell me that I am, is.

Somehow, I'm supposed to learn spells and how to ground myself to the elements, fight the fact that I want him like I want air, and not freak out that my parents are part of a shadow coven trying to pull me over to the dark side.

Yeah. No problem.

START READING CURSED MAGIC TODAY

THE HARBOR POINT SERIES

A new adult contemporary romance series

Meet Gio and Sal.
Two damaged men who meet the woman who can
set them right.

Then there's Cash.
He's not damaged but he's ready to do the healing
when he meets Gemma.

**START READING LOVE BY THE SLICE
TODAY**

THE FALLOUT SERIES

A new adult romance series

Coming home is hard.
Finding out the boy you loved had a baby with your
former best friend… heartbreaking.

START READING LAST GOOD THING TODAY

GAMBLING ON LOVE

A new adult romance series

Desperate times call for desperate measures so
Flannery Tate is selling her virginity.

START READING HIGHEST BIDDER TODAY

I you'd like to just keep up with my sales and new releases, you can follow me on BookBub!

Bookbub: https://www.bookbub.com/authors/heather-young-nichols

Heather Young-Nichols is a USA Today Bestselling author of contemporary and paranormal romances. She writes swoony heroes and snarky heroines with a heap of romance.

When she's not writing, she's binging a show with her kids, watching base-ball, or snuggling with her cuddly animals.

Find Heather on Social Media or by visiting her website.

heatheryoungnichols.com

facebook.com/heatheryoungnicholsauthor
instagram.com/heatheryoungnichols
amazon.com/Heather-Young-Nichols/e/B00KKTM54A
bookbub.com/authors/heather-young-nichols
tiktok.com/@heatheryoungnichols